BONES
OF A
SAINT

BONES

OF ✝ A

SAINT

GRANT FARLEY

Excerpt from "Casey Jones." Words by Robert Hunter. Music by Jerry Garcia.
Copyright © 1970 Ice Nine Publishing Co., Inc. Copyright renewed.
All rights administered by Universal Music Corp. All rights reserved.
Used by permission. Reprinted by permission of Hal Leonard LLC.

Excerpt from "Fly Like an Eagle." Words and music by Steve Miller.
Copyright © 1976 by Sailor Music. Copyright renewed. All rights reserved.
Used by permission. Reprinted by permission of Hal Leonard LLC.

This is a work of fiction. Names, characters, places, and incidents either are the product
of the author's imagination or are used fictitiously, and any resemblance to actual persons,
living or dead, businesses, companies, events, or locales is entirely coincidental.

Published in the United States by Soho Teen
an imprint of Soho Press, Inc.
227 W 17th Street
New York, NY 10011

Library of Congress Cataloging-in-Publication Data
Farley, Grant, 1951- author.
Bones of a saint / Grant Farley.

ISBN 978-1-64129-117-0
eISBN 978-1-64129-118-7

1. Coming of age—Fiction. 2. Gangs—Fiction. 3. Brothers—Fiction. 4. People with
disabilities—Fiction. 5. Secrets—Fiction. 6. California, Northern—History—
20th century—Fiction. I. Title
PZ7.1.F3674 Bon 2020 I DDC [Fic]—dc23 2019041731

Interior design by Janine Agro, Soho Press, Inc.

Printed in the United States of America

10 9 8 7 6 5 4 3 2 1

For Tobey

Caitlin, Erin, and David

Trouble ahead, trouble behind,
And you know that notion just crossed my mind.
—"Casey Jones," The Grateful Dead

They made the devil's sacrifice
Within the devil's temple, wicked wise . . .
—"The Pardoner's Tale," Chaucer

We ask . . . to be transformed into children so that we may one
day enter the Kingdom of Heaven.
—Veneration prayer to St. Jerome Emiliani

BONES

OF A

SAINT

DENIAL

The priest climbed the trail into the foothills as the mission bell tolled matins. Lupine brushed his leg. The path disappeared beneath wild mustard, but he followed from memory. He passed a mound covered in poppies. Purgatory. He was close now. He hiked along the ridge, stopping at the base of the great oak stump, its charred limb poking at the sky. He shrugged off the backpack, pulled out the spade, knelt, and drove the blade into the mud between the roots. Seventeen years. He dug deeper. Why had he waited so long? He had lived as though in a trance. He dug deeper still. Denial, perhaps.

This wooden handle, the dirt beneath it, the charred stump, these felt real even as the images of his own life slipped away. Something tugged at the shovel and his chest tightened. He pulled back on the handle. The blade ripped free, rising above him trailing a shred of blood-encrusted canvas. Again, he thrust the blade into the soil. It clunked metal. He tossed the shovel aside and dug his hands into the earth and grasped the smooth surface. He tried to pray.

Finally, he stood and brushed off his knees, massaged his lower back, and stared down into the valley as it emerged into the soft light.

No hurry now.

He studied the foothills across the valley, their shadows unfolding. The trees rose along the riverbed. He could not see the farmhouse. But he recognized the hill that sheltered it. The children had grown up in that home, but then had left the valley. Had children of their own now. All but him.

As the priest knelt again and reached into the earth, the tale of that summer slid into an eternal present, like a boy's train forever looping upon itself on a figure-eight track.

And always, that voice.

ARCANGEL VALLEY, CALIFORNIA

1978

CHAPTER ONE

CANTE BURY

I'm watching their faces shimmer under the neon blue of the CANTERBURY TRAILER PARK sign that really only hums CANTE BURY with the *e* sort of wiggling on and off. Mr. Sanders would be POed at me for letting the sign go like that, but I don't got the heart to mess with it.

Only three guys are playing over-the-line—Buns Bernie, Ed the Head, and Michael James Bartholomew the Third, who is only MJB to us. They're seventeen and don't want to be bothered with a sawed-off fifteen, but I'm too slick to ditch, so they're sending me to deep, deep center. Under the streetlights, guys can play all night. Buns steps into the batter's box chalked on the asphalt.

The first raindrops hit my face, dripping a low-tide funk. No such thing as a rainout, so I grab my glove. The sign crackles and hums, raindrops waving like fishing line through CANTE BURY.

I see her first. Roxanne's hair is blacker than the twenty-coat paint job on Chaco's Impala. She parts it down the middle and it hangs straight down around her shoulders. In that light, it's an oil-slick blue, and the way the drops bead like a slick wax job, she don't even need a hat. She stares at me with her eyelids drooping.

"Hey, RJ." She says it like I'm some kind of curse. She won't let go that hate between our moms. She slinks up to the older guys, who are froze like Carew checking up on ball four. The chalk lines are bleeding down the gutter, but they sure don't see it.

"Whaturyaguys doing?" Roxanne says in that low voice she thinks is a turn-on. She snaps her gum.

"Playing with our bats," I say. "What does it look like we're doing, Foxy Roxy?"

"Don't be gross."

She turns to the other guys and it don't take a genius to see that where she's taking them she won't let me tag along, not even in deep, deep center.

The rain has slowed to a drizzle.

She trades tongues with them for a while, but they're getting kind of tired of it. Roxanne finally pushes away from MJB, hands him his wireframes she was holding for him, and stands back like she knows she better get past first base or they'll go back to their old game.

"Let's go out to the old Miller place," she whispers.

"That's a Blackjack hangout," Buns says.

"No one's lived there in years," Roxanne says. "I don't see no Blackjack sign on it."

I'm hypnotized by these water drops hanging on the ends of her fake lashes.

"The Blackjacks don't need no sign," Buns says. "Everyone just knows it."

"Yeah," Ed the Head mumbles. There's nothing funkier than that soggy pot stench from his shirt. "No one messes with them. No one."

"Precisely." MJB nods.

"Maybe you boys ain't ready. Maybe you boys just ain't up for a man's game."

I know what kind of game it is she's talking about, but I can't figure why they're turned on by Roxanne.

I stash our gear and tag along as they follow her like three puppy dogs toward the old Miller place. It's supposed to be haunted, if a guy is lame enough to believe any of that stuff. The Millers lost their farm sometime way before I was born, and most of the land has been sold off, so no one is busting butt to buy a house in the middle of nowhere. Rumors are that some city dude bought it, but it's been a couple weeks now and no one's showed. Anyway, no one ever moves to this valley, they only leave. If they're lucky.

It takes most of an hour, but finally the guys are crouching out in the drizzle on a hill and staring down at the shadow of that house. Roxanne and me sit under an oak uphill from them.

"I'll go on reconnaissance." MJB means he'll go make sure no guys from the Blackjacks got dibs on the place tonight. He slides down the hill and we wait.

Finally, we hear his stupid all-clear whistle.

They creep down the hill and in through a broken window and I crawl in right after them. Roxanne Bic-lights a couple candles waxed to the floor. In that glow I see a curved banister torn from the stairs, beer bottles and wrappers scattered across the hardwood, and graffiti scrawled across the walls. There are worse hauntings than plain old ghosts.

"Find us some wood," Roxanne says. "We'll make us a fire." She does this disco spin. "It'll be sooo dee-vine."

The other guys tear around the house. I watch as she squats by the candles with her chin resting on her knees, her feet soaked through her rainbow-colored surfer sandals. She takes a bottle of nail polish out of the back pocket of her tight jeans and the bottle click-clicks as she shakes it. She wipes her toes and smears another coat of that weird red-purple across her toenails. It's like her own color, Foxy Roxy purple. Her head bobs to a soundtrack only she can hear. She spreads her toes and wiggles them like a sea anemone.

The guys stumble back lugging ripped-up baseboards that they toss onto the grate. They stand staring at it. The closest they've ever come to lighting a fireplace is plugging in MJB's red crackling cellophane heater. Roxanne pushes them away and lights it.

I'm standing away from them and don't bother to point out what that smoke might lure, even at night. Especially at night.

The guys step back and watch her. She closes her eyes and stands with her back to the fire, wet hair hanging down. She's wearing flared jeans like us, except hers are hip-huggers, and she's wearing a T-shirt like the rest of us, too. But the fire is crackling behind her and the way she looks under that wet T-shirt, well, that's not like the rest of us. At all. Except maybe Buns on account of he's fat, but that don't count.

Her soundtrack comes moaning out of her now. Something about staying alive. She spins and moans. On the radio the song sounds like a bunch of stoned chipmunks, but drifting from her it's more like a sad, all-alone girl. Her disco spin slows and slows . . .

She sees me and stops.

"I ain't putting on no show for him. It's degrading."

"Man," I say. "You're just POed 'cause Buns got bigger tits than you."

Buns's face turns all purple red, Foxy Roxy purple, but the others don't dare laugh. Buns knows he can't catch me—I'm too slick. They'd spend half the night chasing me around that old house. "Look," MJB says with that fake accent, "there's no need for everyone to get perturbed. Why don't we simply play a little game of Murder with RJ here, then we can get down to it."

Murder is really only hide-and-seek for guys who don't want to look dorky playing a little kid game.

"Oh?" Ed the Head asks. "Ooooh. Got ya."

"You must think I'm a total dork," I say. "You're gonna have me hide, and then it'll be, like, tomorrow before one of you bothers to come looking for me."

It's a standoff.

"The boys wouldn't do that," Roxanne says to me like I'm one of the other guys. "Honey, you and me can hide together, and the others can try and find us."

Well, I figure as long as I got her, they won't be far off. "Okay," I say, "but don't try and rape me or nothing."

"Don't be disgusting," she says.

So the guys start counting to a hundred and I creep for the stairs.

"No, this way," she whispers. She leads me outside. "I know just the place."

"Just the place is upstairs out of the rain," I say.

"That's the first place they'll look."

Right. So I follow her. I know that's dumb, but there's

nothing better than playing Murder around an almost-haunted house in the rain. She sneaks around the side.

There's this stone shed that looks like it sunk in the mud clear to the roof. It's even got this little pipe sticking out that could be a chimney, except it's just an air vent. A root cellar.

"Help me with this." She tries to lift the door, which comes out of the ground at an angle. It's like she's been here before.

We lift the door with this *ka-blang* that if the guys don't hear they got to be deaf. The blackness and the cold slither up the stone steps and there's no way, Jose, that I'm going down there.

"What are you waiting for?" she asks from halfway down the stairs.

"Probably a big, juicy black widow down there."

Then she's standing at the bottom just out of the rain, lighting a cigarette. She almost looks like some starlet the way she's letting out that smoke real slow and leaning on one hip in that wet T-shirt. There's this sweet smell seeping up from her. No bottle smell, this is all her.

The Bic light flickers in that little stone room and it looks just like a place where they bury people in horror movies, only the people are zombies or vampires or something and they come out at night and suck people's necks or eat them—that kind of thing. She flicks an ash. "I didn't know you were chick-en."

There's a log next to the door. A plan slaps into my head. Slam that door shut on her and roll that log over on top of the door and just leave her there. It'd serve her right for all the mean things she done to me over the years. But I don't pay attention to that plan, 'cause when it comes right down to it I wouldn't lock my worst enemy down there. The guys are calling to each other from the house.

Roxanne turns and stares at one of the walls, her eyebrows going up, and she just whispers, "Oh, wow!"

"What is it?"

She's just staring at that wall. "Far freaking out."

"What?"

My feet take me right down the stairs to check it out. Whoever built that room made a big deal about it. Even the floor is solid stone. I look at that wall, but there's only rock and some spiderwebs that probably are from black widows. There's a creak and then *ka-BLANG* and then blackness. I can't believe I fell for that.

I turn and feel for the door through the cobwebs, pounding and shouting, "Let me ouuut!"

Her whispers bounce all around the stones. I turn. Some of the night seeps in through the air vent. I hear her scuffle right on the roof next to it. She's there. Crouched. Waiting to hear me.

"Let me out and I'll just go home."

"I don't believe you."

Nothing else to say.

"Look," she says, "as soon as I'm done with those guys, we'll come back and let you out."

I yell some more, but she's gone. Then it hits me. She planned for this to happen. I sit in the middle of the floor trying not to think of Father Speckler and the way he used to lock me in that coat closet at Our Lady's. A six-footer could reach out his arms and touch both walls, but my arms are wrapped around me. The room is so still and cold that I can't even shiver. *Hail Mary, full of grace.* I know that some fat black widow is right over my head, dropping into my hair like a loogie. *The Lord is with thee.* I'm rocking back and forth, back and forth, just doing the Hail Marys and listening to the rain against the metal vent and smelling the old stone. *Blessed art thou among women.*

I don't know how long I'm here, my body as light as a dried-up leaf swirling above that stone floor. The walls spreading out . . . and out . . . and out . . . to blackness like forever and I know I'm dying and that if someone don't open this freaking door real soon and reach down and lift me out of this black place, then I will be dead. Forever and ever.

Then I hover in that blackness, listening like I'm an outsider with my ear pressed up against the world. Like lying on that coat closet floor listening to Father Speckler doing one of his *we're all God's children* numbers on the class.

Rain brushes the trees. Roxanne giggles and then sings about that staying alive . . . A tree claws the side of the out-buildings. Car tires crunch on gravel.

Blackjacks?

The car door slams. Heavy boots slide on the porch. Roxanne screams from inside the house. The guys yell. Then this weird, twisted kind of shout that's got to be a man from the car. Doors slam. Then lots of running, first on wood and then on mud and grass. Someone runs right by the cellar. I suck that big breath, ready to let loose a scream, but a voice in my head whispers, *Shut the hell up.* The only sound now is the faraway gong of the mission bell blown by the wind.

Then silence. Not a soul. I might be trapped here forever.

Then shuffling footsteps near the cellar. Circling the cellar. One foot dragging behind the other across the wet grass and mud. Not a Blackjack. It stops near the air vent. All kinds of weird thoughts slap through me, like *What if it's my father's ghost?* Then I'm not floating. I'm just huddled on that stone floor with the cold pressing all around me. Pressing. Pressing! And it just squeezes out of me. "Let me out! Please let me out!"

"Someone down there?" Instead of shouting, it's a hoarse wheeze. "Someone down there?"

My breath slides around the stones.

The foot drags along to the door. The sound of the log plopping over on the wet grass. The door lifts, a peek of night slipping in, and then slams back. More heavy breathing. The door lifts again and crashes open and the night floods in.

A worn black boot clumps on the first stair.

I'm holding my breath.

The flashlight beam blinds me. Beyond the light is something red, shriveled . . . a hand reaching down at me . . . It's so old, like a skeleton's maybe.

Like a claw.

I push up out of that cellar, brushing past this . . . this old man . . . a stench of something sweetly sick . . . out into the rain . . . running . . . slipping in the mud . . . up and running.

Freeee.

God, I run.

CHAPTER TWO

CANNIBALS

I'm trudging to the top of a hill in that muggy heat, my brother clinging to my back. Charley has this way of wrapping his legs around my waist and his arms around my neck so that he weighs no more than a backpack. He knows that one day he'll be too big and I'll drop his sorry ass for good. Then I whiff wet grass and I'm back to last week . . . *pushing up out of that cellar, brushing past that ancient-looking dude, a stench of something sweetly sick . . . running . . . slipping in the mud . . .*

Cellar. Cell. Cave. Crypt. I know all the words. I read how some monks spend their lives holed up searching for God. But there's no way. No freaking way to hear Him through stone.

A truck horn blasts behind me, but I don't look back. Nino-'n-Smitty's flatbed with the stake gates whines up the hill, clunks a gear, and passes me with Smitty riding shotgun, his head out the window like a dog and his stringy beard blowing in the wind. The Dead blast from the 8-track:

Driving that train, high on cocaine, Casey Jones you better watch your speed . . .

Smitty's tattooed arm dangles on the door and slaps the beat against the metal.

Trouble ahead, lady in red, take my advice you're better off dead.

He waves at me and grins as the truck tops the hill, puking exhaust in my face. Migrants are grabbing those truck gates so they won't fall out the open back. They won't hear no *ranchera* from Nino-'n-Smitty. A guy grins from the shade of a flat straw hat and points at us, and the others laugh. Then the truck slides down the grade.

Manny's house floats in the ground fog down in the hollow.

"Okay, Big Foot, it's downhill from here. You can walk."

Charley straightens his tie and follows me. He can talk, but he hardly ever feels like it. His white dress shirt and tie don't go with the blue jeans, but he always wears the same jeans, ironed, with a two-inch cuff on the left leg, and the right leg slit neatly so it hangs to the ground over the huge right shoe. The tie is for the Corpus Christi Festival near Mission San Miguel Arcangel. Since he just did first Communion, he gets to be in this little flower procession. He's been practicing extra hard on his walking. That festival is pretty cool when you think about it, a bunch of normal people acting like cannibals chomping on God.

I sniff my black T-shirt to check the funk. Then I follow Charley down the hill. Manny's place could be a for real farm if his dad ever tried. But the fields are just dead weeds now. The only animals are chickens that lay wherever they feel like so that Manny and me got Easter all year round trying to find the eggs, and a half dozen sorry pigs that get the eggs if we don't. There's a real house that's hardly bigger than my trailer, with this satellite dish out front that's near half as big as the house. Since Manny's mom died, his dad just sits and watches sports.

Maria and Adelita are sitting on the front porch ratting their hair. Their tits look fine through those peasant blouses. I don't feel sorry anymore for Manny having one younger and three older sisters. Charley hobbles up the steps and sits between them and they start making their fuss over him and I wouldn't mind trading places with him, wouldn't mind at all. People think he's delicate, the way he looks like one of those porcelain dolls at Mrs. Elliot's Antiques and Collectibles Emporium. These blue veins web through his skin like the cracks on those dolls. But Charley, he's as tough as they come.

I turn and head to the back screen porch. The migrants have slipped away, and Nino-'n-Smitty are already kicking back on beach chairs, a six-pack between them, under the scrawny oak that Manny and me call the killing tree. No pig hangs from it today, but there's a whiff of old blood from the clawed bathtub sitting in the shadows behind them. Nino has the same snake tattoo as Smitty, but it looks smaller on his thick arm. Nino is Manny's blood uncle. Smitty isn't blood, but he's his uncle just the same. It's sort of like they're from one of Abuelita's tales that Manny squeezes into English for me. Two halves. One dude.

"Hey, *hermano*!" Nino calls to me.

I hop up the porch steps and slip through the screen door.

Manny gives me our newest greeting: "Aren't you a little short for a storm trooper?"

I answer: "It's the uniform."

We saber-swoosh.

I plop down next to Manny on the wicker.

A smell of beans simmering in cast iron always fills that room. Abuelita stands in front of this Mexican dude, his face scrunched up in pain. Her face is soft skin folds. She rolls up this piece of paper into a funnel and holds it to the dude's ear. She lights a match with her thumbnail and holds it to the funnel all in one slick move.

"Aaaiieee!" The dude cries and lifts his hand to rub the ear and Abuelita slaps the hand away. He nods and grins, the pain gone, as she shows him out the door.

I glimpse Theresa, who is only a year younger than us, back in the kitchen. She used to tie her hair in pigtails with barrettes, but now it's a ribboned ponytail falling to her butt. Then the kitchen door closes.

Well, Abuelita is Manny's grandma, not mine. But I've sort of adopted her. She grabs her mug of cinnamon coffee off the table and heads for us. She always wears a black dress and these thick black shoes that clunk on the hollow floor. She grabs a chair and sits down facing us and puts the glass on the window ledge and lets out this sigh like she's too old and too tired to put up with my *mierda*.

Then she puts her hands on her knees and leans back like she's going to start one of her tales. Her tales are about funny people, the earth and sky, animals that talk, and even witches, what she calls *brujas*. She tells them in Spanish with this soothing singsong and Manny does his best squeezing them into English for me. When we were little we'd listen for hours. I wait, staring out at the world gone brittle through old screens.

But instead of starting a tale, she pulls her chair closer and stares into me. Under the cinnamon coffee breath, she has this purplish old-lady smell that I like. The way Abuelita's brow scrunches up, I'm figuring my own BO must be pretty funky after all. She stares over at Manny and then back at me. She's probably wondering for the hundredth time whether she really wants her *mijo* hanging out with me. But it's years too late to get second thoughts about that.

"This summer, it is going to be full of . . . aye . . . *malevolencia* . . . not so easy for you, Richard James. You will have the big choice to make."

"Full of . . . evil," Manny whispers.

Anyone but Abuelita saying it, and I'd be thinking it was just part of a show. But coming from her, it freezes my insides. I'm seeing back to that root cellar . . . *something red, shriveled, a claw . . . a stench like something sweet, dead . . .*

My mind slips back, escaping to a safer place, the day Manny and me met in the first grade when the nuns lined up the class by height for the fire drill and we punched at each other to decide who was the shortest, earning the glory of marching last in line. We fought at the end of lines through the next couple grades until Abuelita shamed us into stopping by telling us stories of Coyote, who jacked his friends with his mean, sneaky ways. Even though we haven't fought since then, we've stayed best friends. We're sort of the same but opposite, what Mr. Sanders called a paradox. I'm cursed with freckly skin, while he gets brown the color of the mission pews. I got what Mom calls an auburn mop, and he gets straight black hair tied in a cool ponytail like an Indian. I'm skinny and he's fat. I've got five younger sibs and he's got four sisters. I lost my dad when I was three and his sister Theresa killed their mom just getting born . . .

"Come on, Manny. We got to take Charley to his festival."

He shrugs and follows me out around the house to the porch. The sisters are gone, but Charley sits smiling.

"Come on, Big Foot."

We could be riding bikes. Charley can do that if we go slow. But Manny won't ride since the time he was sideswiped near the Banzai. It don't matter that we're not going in that direction now. He still won't ride.

Manny, Charley, and me are halfway to the Mission for Corpus Christi when Buns Bernie, MJB, and Ed the Head are standing by the road. I haven't seen them since that night in the cellar. Something isn't right. If it wasn't for Charley hanging on my back, I'd take off. They'd never catch Manny or me.

"Hey." I nod like everything's cool and push past, except Buns is in front of me like a wall of Jell-O.

"Hey yourself." Buns stares down at me.

I drop Charley to the ground. "So, what's up?"

"You're coming with us."

Maybe I can clown my way out of this. I wave my hand in front of him and chant: "These are not the dudes you're looking for."

I glance at Manny and we both crack up.

"The Blackjacks want to see you."

We're not laughing no more. My legs go weak. No point running even if I could. Then Charley goes still, his eyes staring into space as he finds that place inside that seems to make him invisible to strangers. It's like his own superpower or something.

"Where?" I gulp.

"Up there." Buns points across to the hills edging the

valley. We can't see it from here, but we all know he's pointing to Dead Man's Gorge. No one is allowed up there unless he's Blackjack.

Ed the Head and MJB are silent like the place is some kind of freaking shrine.

"So why would the Ace want me?"

"The Blackjacks are POed at that old city dude for buying the Miller place. He stole their best flatland hangout. And worse, he's an outsider. You and that freak are connected since he's the one that let you out of that root cellar."

"What? How'd they know about that?" Was he really just some old dude? I couldn't say for sure, but he seemed like a hell of a lot more than that.

Buns shrugs.

"You told them," I answer my own question. What had Abuelita said? *Malea . . . mal . . . ?* "So what's it got to do with you three?"

"You ask too many questions," Buns says.

I wait him out.

"You're a part of our initiation."

"You guys Blackjacks? Don't make me laugh."

"Come on," Buns orders.

"Wait. No point in Charley coming. He can't make that climb, you know that."

Ed the Head looks away from me and sucks air like he's toking. MJB cleans his wireframes. But Buns just crosses his arms and stares at me.

"Charley is on his way to the Corpus Christi Festival." I rush on before Buns can slip in a no: "He's in the procession. You can't make him miss that. It's like a sin against God."

"Oh, crap," Ed the Head groans. His family is lapsed, and

they're almost always the most afraid of God's wrath. "Let Charley go."

"You think I'm stupid?" Buns demands. "It's Thursday. Church is on Sunday."

"Well," I say, "this festival is on Thursday, and there ain't nothing you can do about that."

"He's right," Ed says.

"We got our orders," Buns says. "Charley comes, too."

He's making Charley come 'cause he's figured out the best way to get to me is through my brother. Buns has hated me since even before I said that stuff about him and Roxanne's tits.

"Okay, then why Manny?"

"Ace did not say anything about this other fellow," MJB says. "He may even be perturbed at us for bringing unauthorized personnel."

Buns is trying so hard to figure it all out that his face is scrunched up like he's constipated.

"If you're going, RJ, then I'm going," Manny says.

That's the bravest words I ever heard anyone say. Man, what a long, strange trip *this* will be.

CHAPTER THREE

BLACKJACKS

We're hiking up the foothills to Dead Man's Gorge just so we can worship some psycho stoner they call the Ace. Buns goes first. I follow with Charley hanging on, clutching my neck. Manny is right behind me. MJB is after him, making sure we don't get second thoughts. Finally, Ed the Head huffs and puffs back where we don't have to whiff his homegrown. Mr. Sanders would've called us a pilgrimage.

We climb the trail into the foothills, and I can see clear across the valley to the hills we call Big Mama. They look like a lady lying along the coastals with huge jugs sticking straight up in the sky, just like she was getting a for real tan. Which is funny since her weeds are just starting to turn brown for summer. The shadows even give her some soft skin folds.

My T-shirt is already soaked with sweat where Charley is hanging on. We march along and my stomach hollows as I remember all the Blackjack rumors. Beatings. Hazings.

Robbery. Protection. Drugs. Rape. And murder. There could be bodies buried up here going back a hundred years, clear back to Coyote Jack himself.

The Blackjacks hardly ever get caught, and never once convicted. No one climbs up here uninvited. No one. And no one dares to testify. Years go by. Faces grow up and then leave. Some of them find their way out of the valley. Others melt in with those that went before and then become a part of our little world. But there's always new boys to replace them. There's always the Blackjacks.

A whistle skips down at us from way up Dead Man's Gorge. It's got to be some kind of lame signal. I feel this slimy kind of honor to be climbing into this darkest place.

We reach the top of the ridge and walk along a trail with the whole valley there below us. Those farm and machinery buildings look like metal dice tossed across the fields. In an hour they'll be floating in heat waves.

Buns stops again. He's pointing to a rockslide below the trail. The earth humps up like some kind of big animal is buried there. Buns picks up a stone and throws it. It makes a hollow thud against the mound, kind of like hurling rocks at the old water tower on Mission. My stomach flips just hearing a sound, like that coming up out of the ground.

"See that latch there?" Buns has that low voice guys use when telling stories, like about the ghost with the golden arm.

A metal latch sticks its head out of that hump of rocks. It's all peeling yellow and rust. There's a padlock clamped to it.

"It's one of them old water trailers like the farmers used to use," Ed the Head says, messing up Buns's story.

"Right," Buns says. "But no one knows how it got up here. It's a mystery like those giant stones over in New York."

"England," MJB says.

"Whatever. It's some kind of mystery only the Ace knows about. If someone messes up, they get locked in there until he decides their punishment. He calls it purgatory."

"Sounds to me like that *is* the punishment. Come on, let's get this over with." I push past Buns with Charley still on my back. The hot air wiggles on top of the rocks and dead weeds, and I'm feeling dizzy.

I climb over a rise and that huge oak tree is there maybe a football field ahead of us. Of course, I've never seen it before. Well, maybe I caught the shadow of the tip-top branches one time when I telescoped it from far below, Manny not daring to even put his eyeball to the lens. It's the oldest, biggest living thing in the whole valley. Its branches spread like creepy fingers against that empty sky.

I almost step on three guys lying in the shade of a boulder. One of them is Bobby Martin. He's just a year older than me. We used to hang out together. Most of the time, he'd been an okay guy, like when he'd share his Twinkie at lunch. But then he'd do something gross like take insects or lizards or mice and put them in coffee cans and then drop in a firecracker. One day he found this litter of kittens up in the hills. It was his find of a lifetime, and I knew there was no way to talk or even punch him out of it. So I told him to go for the Lady Finger firecrackers and I'd watch the kittens until he got back. Of course, by the time he got back, me and the kittens were gone. After that we hated each other. I hadn't seen him in a couple years, mostly 'cause he went to Our Lady's, which I'd got kicked out of. It only takes one look to see that the bad part of him has taken hold and there's nothing left of that guy who'd share his last Twinkie.

"Come on, what are you waiting for?" Buns has slipped by me while I'm spaced out.

I step past Bobby and we pretend we don't know each other. All the time I'm seeing that oak tree through the corner of my eye. Three guys could spread their arms out wide and not even reach around its trunk. There are two huge roots, each split down the middle sort of like a goat or pig foot. Like the tree is just toeing that dried-up dirt to keep from falling over the edge. It's still a good fifty yards off, but I don't want to look at it, so I'm checking out the younger guys sitting in the shade of a boulder. Some of them can't be more than eleven or twelve. They must be what the Blackjacks call the Deuces.

If you're a Blackjack, you live at home, go to school, or have a job in the valley, but this place gets inside you. This place is where you hang for real.

Platforms are nailed to a couple stumpy oaks, with sixteen- or seventeen-year-olds dangling their legs over, staring down at us. They're the Jokers. They just watch as we pass.

Manny is beside me now.

A narrow gorge cuts into the hill, and a camp has been set up with a big tent and pup tents and a campfire and ice chests and all kinds of cool stuff. The older guys live up here for weeks at a time in the summer. It makes me sick seeing this awesome hangout twisted into something creepy.

Manny is trying to look cool, but he's shaking. I punch his shoulder. He manages a grin.

"*Sí, se puede,*" he says.

Don't know what that means except it's got to do with the farm workers. Nino says it, so it must be cool. I nod.

We pass the camp and as I get closer I see where the trunk of that huge tree was hit by lightning a long time ago. Two smaller trunks grow out of that black stump. At the bottom the trunks look okay, but then they start twisting with these black sort of veins running through them, like the bad part is creeping into the new. The guys kicking back near that shade are the oldest and meanest yet. My back is so slick with sweat now that Charley is choking me just trying to keep from sliding off. I stop at the edge of the shade. Charley slides down.

"Don't go in there," Manny says.

I glance at Charley and squint my eyes, hoping he'll catch the signal and do his invisible thing, but he's too scared.

I feel my feet stepping into the shadows. It's dead quiet. The air don't move at all so that it feels all stuffy and even hotter than out in the sun. No one dared nail a platform to this tree. There's one of those rattan chairs with the fan backs set deep in the shade between the roots. The Ace has one leg of his old jeans over the arm of the chair with his cracked and muddy cowboy boot just dangling. His elbow is on the other arm of the chair, with his chin resting on his fist. He's wearing a torn T-shirt and a Raiders cap. He don't look any real age, but stories have the Ace as twenty-one. The way he just sits there, he almost looks like an old puppet waiting for someone to pull on the strings.

Most of the other older boys I've seen somewhere over the years in this valley, like at school or working some nothing job or just hanging out. But I've never laid eyes on this guy. Still, I got this feeling like I should know him.

"I thought you'd be bigger," the Ace says.

"Yeah, me too," I say.

His lip goes up in a kind of jagged grin. "How old are you, RJ?"

"Sixteen."

"Don't jerk me. You're fifteen."

"If you know so much, how come you asked?"

His eyelid twitches. It's the only thing that moves, but it's a tell that says, *You'll pay for every smart-ass thing you say.* So I shut up.

"Fifteen and already you got a rep." He just sits there like he expects me to thank him or something.

A guy sits on each side of him, each with long, stringy hair wrapped in bandana headbands. The one on the left has gray hair like an old man, except he's no more than twenty. They wear the same boots and jeans and all that, but they for sure don't own the Ace's power.

He pulls off the Raiders cap. His head is just freckles and stubble and sweat, which he rubs away with his hand. He wipes the sweat off on his jeans and puts back the cap. His eyes drill into me. "You know how long there's been Blackjacks?"

I shrug.

"Always."

So what can I say to that?

"This was Coyote Jack's hideout," he says.

Even though I've heard all this before, I sure don't interrupt. The Blackjacks might have all this lame poker stuff in their names, but the real guy Coyote Jack goes back way before any of that.

"There's been Blackjacks on this here spot for over a hundred years. The posse tracked Coyote and his riders after they slaughtered those people at the mission for their forty-niner gold. They trapped him right where you're standing and hung the old half-breed from this tree."

I'd heard that, too. Who hadn't? I'd even heard the stories of his gold buried around here.

"Let me tell you something." He leans forward like he's telling a secret, but that's just for show 'cause he wants the others to hear, too. "Ol' Coyote Jack, he ain't never left here."

The eye twitches. I wait for him to flip one last card. "That freak is moving into the old Miller place. Even as we sit here, moving trucks are unloading some of the sweetest antiques you ever saw. Like he thinks that place is his. Can you believe that? Hell, what kind of an outsider, an old geeze, would want to move here? That place is ours. No one takes from the Blackjacks. No one. That old man *owes* us. We got plans for him. And you're gonna be part of the plans."

He takes the hat off and rubs his head. It's a regular habit. He picks up a stick and draws something that looks kind of like a star.

"Study it. It's a pentagram." It don't take a whole lot of studying, but I got practice from school making a pretend study face, so I go along with it. "You will make that sign three times, at midnight, inside that old man's house. Make them big, real big."

Sounds kind of lame, so I just nod.

"And these other two, they go with you."

Any arguing now will just make it worse.

"What do I make the sign with?"

"Blood."

CHAPTER FOUR

WINDOWPANE

I'm washing the dishes and staring through the porthole of our Silverstream trailer and imagining I'm in a spaceship and that those moonlit fields are some alien lunarscape. I feel the walls trembling and the Silverstream rising and hovering, and then blasting off for a universe without Blackjacks. Yeah, right. After I clean the kitchenette, the teak glows and the chrome shines.

Mom has the swing shift tonight. Peanut is already asleep in the bedroom she shares with her, which was originally the living room. I squeeze past the bathroom to the other end of the trailer, where Amy and the twins share the one for real bedroom. Everything inside the trailer is pull-down or built-in.

They are already curled in their beds waiting for my story. Amy has the built-in bed with the dresser drawers beneath it. Across from her, StevieandSuzy get the bunks. I'm working up a story so scary that they'll end up scrunched against the wall so that no monsters will claw their toes. Amy stares at me, ready for any tale I throw at her, while her cat Peabody purrs beside her. I don't even feel guilty because my scary stories are make-believe. They help them escape the for real scary. A whole flying saucer full of bloodsucking aliens is nothing compared to a single Blackjack.

"Where was I?" I ask them. They're wide-eyed and don't answer. "Oh yeah. So, these hairy, spidery humanoids scuttled out of their caves and crept down into the little kingdom. Now, the old wizard knew of these poisonous creatures, and he summoned the boy . . ." As the story builds, the twins curl into the shadows at the back of their bunks. "The wizard casts a spell on the boy, granting him the power to fly . . ."

They're asleep before I get to the part with the zombie peasants. Except for Peabody. His green eyes stare through me. That cat and me go way back.

I step out the rounded door that is the Silverstream's entrance, and down into the wood-framed room that runs along the side of the trailer. This room is a combination living room and boys' bedroom. Charley and me sleep on pull-out sofas. I don't pull mine out because the cushions are more comfortable, especially now that they're worn down to the shape of my body and they cup around me like a cloud. I pull one of Peanut's plastic baby bottles from under a cushion and sit down.

Charley is lying under his Snoopy blanket and watching the late-night news, which usually puts him to sleep. For real stories don't scare him. The television flashes a view of the front of a courthouse, people everywhere. Then a newscaster's voice announces that Son of Sam has been sentenced. Twenty-five years for each of the six known murders.

"That's one hundred and fifty years, Charley, which about covers it. Math don't lie."

Charley nods, but it's because he's about to fall asleep.

"He had millions of people in New York hiding their toes at night, but he didn't make one difference here, in this valley. Evil is sort of like a piece of gum. The farther you stretch it, the thinner it gets."

Charley don't answer.

"What happened to Harvey, you think?"

"Who's Harvey?" Charley mumbles.

"During the trial, the Son of Sam said his neighbor's dog, Harvey, ordered him to do all the murders. I wonder about that dog."

The newscasters don't say nothing about Harvey. Instead, there's a closing story about Christa Tybus of London setting a world record of twenty-four and a half hours for the hula-hoop, and as the newscasters chuckle over that, I punch off the tube.

Charley is asleep.

I can't sleep, so I get up, kicking the baby bottle, and I'm out the door and into the warm night.

I flop down in my beach chair, bathing in the blue glow of that neon arch humming CANTE BURY. It's where I go to get answers. Or not. The chair sits on the empty slab that once held Mr. Sanders's trailer. No one slaps a trailer down here no more because renters say the place is haunted. But it's not ghost haunted, and I should know. I wish it really was ghost haunted. Wish I could hear his voice on the breeze, howling at me for letting his sign go, but then forgiving me. And then telling me what I should do tomorrow.

I take out the Hohner harmonica, which is all that Dad left

me. I suck in the warm air and blow out, notes rattling the night. His dress uniform hangs in Mom's cubby closet and his triangled flag lies under her bed. He could at least have left me something cool, like a bayonet or an unloaded pistol. Even some war medals. I blow sound out and snap it back like bubblegum.

Nino-'n-Smitty say war killed my dad. I don't know how that's true because he came home after, and he married Mom and they had me and he lived until I was three. When I was almost old enough, they also told me that he had been killed by Windowpane, which is LSD, and I thought there must be a window somewhere where I could see my dad on the other side. Father Speckler tried to con me into thinking that was heaven, but I don't buy it. I never seen such a for real window. So my dad couldn't have died in war. But Mr. Sanders, he said there are all kinds of ways war kills people.

No tune. Just in and out. The taste of metal. *Pentagrams*, that's what the Ace ordered. In and out. Clicking my tongue on the wood slats. *Blood.*

That old man at the Miller place is beyond creepy, and I don't want to get caught by him, but how bad could he hurt the rest of my family? Why did he even come here? Is he like one of those old elephants on *Wild Kingdom* that go off somewhere far away to die? That's about all he's got left to do. Die. That and maybe kill people and bury them in his cellar.

The Blackjacks, on the other hand, could crush everyone I love. Laughing the whole time. I will be doing a bad thing tagging those pentagrams. If I get busted, then I'll get sentenced to a million summers of juvie camp digging fire breaks. But that don't compare to a single day of atonement to the Blackjacks if I don't do it.

The lesser of two evils. We can sneak in there, tag the walls, get out. A one-time thing. I don't know how the Blackjacks will know we've done it, but they have their ways. Younger boys as lookouts, maybe. So it's not a queston of *if*. It's *how*. How to get enough blood. How to carry that blood. How to carry all the brushes or stuff to spread the blood. How to get out again without getting caught.

I watch our trailer sitting there in the dark, the sibs safe and fast asleep. I should be weaning Peanut off the plastic bottles and onto juice cups, but I'm too lazy. Then the answer hits me. *The how.* And once I see the first how, the rest start to fall into place. I snap out one last note and then suck it back in, and then put the Hohner in my pocket.

Maybe. Just maybe I really can do this.

CHAPTER FIVE

BARF VADER

It's still two hours to sunset, but the light is already fading behind the high, snotty fog. Plastic clunks from inside my backpack. Manny's front porch is empty of any sisters, which is a good sign for what we got to do.

I round the corner to the back. A dead pig hangs from the killing tree. It's Barf Vader, the mean pig from the dark side. Blood drips from his throat into the clawed bathtub. Nino-'n-Smitty are standing around that tub drinking Buds like it was a campfire.

I hop up the back steps and onto the screened porch. There's a table made out of two big doors on sawhorses that takes up half the room. It seems there's always someone at that eating table, and half the time it's people I don't even know. But today it's only Manny. The porch is dark and cool.

"You're a little short for a storm trooper," he says.

"It's the uniform," I answer.

We saber-swoosh, but our hearts aren't in it no more.

"You missed 'Buelita sticking the pig," Manny says.

"No, I didn't miss it," I say.

He starts to say something but then looks at me and shuts up. Manny is wearing black jeans and a black tee just like me. "So, where's Charley?"

"We'll pick him up on the way." The backpack makes plastic thunks as I drop it and take a Fresca from the old fridge. "It's too much of a pain having to haul blood and him at the same time."

"Why don't we just leave him out of this," Manny says.

"The Ace said all three of us." I pop the can and chugalug half "Anyway, no better lookout than Charley."

"But what if we gotta run for it . . ." His voice trails off.

"We could ride the Stingrays," I say.

"No way," he says.

"Why not?" I know why not, and I feel mean even as I'm saying it. "We ain't going near the Banzai."

Manny squints at the backpack. "That don't sound like paintbrushes."

"Ain't." I crush the empty can and toss it at the trash bag in the corner, glad to get the Stingray problem out of the way. "I got a better idea."

"Oh man," he groans. "I don't even wanna hear it."

"Baby bottles," I say.

"Baby bottles?"

"Baby bottles."

"That's your better idea."

"Think about it. We just scoop the blood into these plastic baby bottles, see. We can carry it in the backpack so no one would even know. When we get into the old man's house, we just pull out the bottles, squirt the walls, and we're gonzo. We don't mess up furniture or nothing."

"I won't even ask where you got the bottles."

"Man, they're popping out of furniture all over the trailer, and Peanut won't need them no more."

I stare out back. A yellow light bulb hangs by an extension cord from the tree, throwing a creepy light around that pig. I can see Nino's green tattoo slithering up his arm. That tattoo would swallow up most arms whole, but it's just a snake on him. His huge bare chest is slick with sweat. He wears his jeans low under his beer belly, so in back you can see the scars and the top of his crack. The jeans hang down like an empty bag. He has a low, hoarse kind of voice, but it carries over the others.

Abuelita carries a tray from the kitchen. She drops plates in front of us with homemade sausages the size of pancakes. One whiff says they could burn a hole through your tongue. Manny digs in. I stare out at that pig, then down at my plate. Then back at that pig. Abuelita just wipes her hands on the apron and watches me. I don't make a move at that sausage.

"Your brother, you still do the care of his feet as I taught you?" she asks.

"Yeah . . . well, sometimes . . . sort of," I lie.

I look away from her stare. Whenever that memory comes at me, it's the smells I remember first . . . Charley's scabs oozing a stench kind of like an anthill. Then the warm water in the plastic tub a swirl of salt and baking soda and rosemary and other stuff.

"You take the time and dry and rub as I show you?"

"Sort of . . ." No point lying to her. "But what's the

use? Those toes ain't never the same. They swell, they melt together, they rub his shoes in different spots so he's always got new blisters. Nothing helps."

"Does he like?"

"Yeah, I guess."

She picks up the plate of sausage.

"Tiene los dedos de un santo." She turns and walks back to the kitchen.

"Manny, what did she say?"

"She said he has . . . uh . . . he has the toes of a saint."

"What's that supposed to mean?"

Manny just shrugs.

Smitty laughs at something Nino said. I look out through the screen and even clear across the yard I see Smitty's Adam's apple jump. If a giant took Nino and rolled him long and skinny like a piece of clay, that's Smitty. He looks like he's wearing a shirt even though he's not. His arms are sort of mud brown, but where the shirt should start he's so white, like Nino says, you need sunglasses to look at him. Smitty's got the same tattoo, except it covers his whole arm. Nino-'n-Smitty have been best buddies since grade school, through 'Nam, through being bikers, to now, when they share a house even though Smitty is married.

"I'll bet Nino-'n-Smitty could kick ass on the Blackjacks." I say it like it's no big deal, but I look close at Manny. A part of me is hoping that all we got to do is tell Nino-'n-Smitty about how the Blackjacks are messing with us. Then, Nino-'n-Smitty, they'll march straight up that hill to that tree and kick butt on all of them.

"Maybe." Manny shrugs and stuffs his face with a tamal. Manny thinks Nino-'n-Smitty can do most anything, but the way he says *maybe* and shrugs, I know that one thing he don't think they can do is kick ass on the Blackjacks.

"Yeah, maybe," I say, the air sort of going out of me, leaving a sick, empty feeling. I know we won't tell about our connection to the Blackjacks to nobody we like. We don't want them to try and help and then get hurt.

Nino-'n-Smitty head for their truck. I grab the pack and we wander out back like we got nothing better to do. We come at that tub in a roundabout way like they say. We move to the far side and I let the backpack slide behind it out of sight.

Flies are already swarming, big hairy bluebottles. Manny waves at them without touching the pig. This thick, coppery sort of smell seeps up at me, and I try not to take big whiffs.

"You be lookout," I say. Barf Vader hangs between me and the house, but we're still out in the open. There's a fly crawling right across the eyeball.

I bend over out of sight behind the tub and grab one of the plastic bottles from the bag. Manny kicks me, and when I come back up three of his sisters have rounded the house and are heading for the screened porch. Two of them just keep going for the porch, but Theresa turns and walks at us, this big grin on her face. Her dark brown hair is razored bangs, not flared out like her wannabe disco sisters'.

"What are you guys doing?"

"Nothing." I shrug.

"This area ain't for girls," Manny says.

She stops, but I think it's more the smell and the sound of blood dripping than anything Manny says.

"I think it's kinda cute," she says.

"Cute?" Manny asks.

Theresa is about the last person who'd call a dead pig hanging from a tree dripping blood into a tub "cute."

"Yeah. I think it's cute the way you stand out here pretending you're Nino-'n-Smitty. *Ninito-y*–little Smitty." She turns, giggling, and heads for the house.

"We ain't pretending nothing," Manny calls.

I'm hypnotized by the way she walks and I can't figure why I never noticed before the way her butt curves out like that, just below her bouncing ponytail.

"Why did you have to have a kid sister who is taller than us?"

"She's only a year younger," Manny says. "And no more than an inch taller. Anyway, it's not her fault. Look at the flip side—it's us who are *shorter* than her."

"Now!" Manny elbows me. "No one is looking."

I hold my breath and bend over the tub with the bottle. A couple of flies are sitting right on the scum. It's kind of like scooping into a bowl of moldy red pudding. The scummy part sticks to my hands, and I almost gag as I stand up and take a breath. I bend down behind the tub and twist on the top. I don't even bother to wipe off the bottle as I drop it in.

After the last bottle is filled, I shoulder the backpack and we beat it for the road, the bottles making thunking and swushing sounds.

With that high fog, there is no sunset. The light just kind of fades out and we're walking along in the dark, not even knowing for how long. Then the fog starts to glow, like around the edges, and we know the full moon is creeping up over the hills.

"What's the point of all this?" Manny asks. "Why the Blackjacks want to tag that old man's house?"

"A warning, maybe."

"Warning of what? What do you think they'll do to him? . . . To us?"

"Don't know." I shrug. "Not even sure the Ace knows for sure. They're just mean to be mean."

"Yeah, I guess. But there's got to be some kind of plan to it all."

"I think this blood is more like a dog pissing to leave its mark. That old geeze has crossed some border with them. No more sense to it than that."

"This is gonna sound weird, RJ, but I wish there was a plan to it. Then a guy knows what he's up against."

I don't need a picture to know what the Blackjacks will do to us if we chicken out, but I'm seeing that old man's red shriveled face and his hands twisted into claws. What will happen if he catches us?

"Let's get Charley and get this over with."

CHAPTER SIX

CREATURE

Manny is lugging the old backpack with the baby bottles filled with blood. The outline of his black tee bounces ahead of me almost like it's day because the night is lunarnescent with the full moon shining through all that fog. I lug Charley.

We climb to the top of the hill and there it is. The lights are off and the windows stare up at us like bug eyes. All that fancy wood like on the porch and around the windows just sits there rotting like Tia Socorro's teeth. Manny sets down the backpack. I set down Charley. All I can hear is our heavy breathing and the slosh of blood against plastic.

Manny stands there staring, so it's up to me.

"Let's do it." I start down the hill. Charley can walk that far, at least. I don't want his extra burden right then.

"So maybe the old man's not asleep," Manny whispers.

I don't answer. The creature that opened the root cellar door on me didn't look the type to sleep nights. I'm listening to the almost-sounds of that fog squeaking up under the warped shingles, sliding along the cracked paint, feeling up the oil casing on that broke-down tractor.

"This way." I don't like the idea, but the best way to sneak up to that house is between the root cellar and the outbuilding. We reach what's supposed to be a barn. Sound drifts from somewhere on the other side. From that root cellar.

"What's that?" Manny asks.

I stop at the corner. The noise is creepier than any fog. It's the old man's wobbly voice, about as cold and dry as that night is warm and wet. Some kind of chant or song. His voice cracking and wobbling and coughing. It's not English or Spanish. The Church don't do Latin no more, but that's my guess. Then the sound stops.

I poke my head around the corner.

The cellar door is shut. The log is gone, replaced by a new latch with a big open padlock. Mumbling echoes inside the cellar. All a guy has to do is flick the latch back over the door and snap that lock. No problem. So why don't I do it? Well, as long as he's down there, maybe we don't need to lock it. The only way to the house, though, is past that root cellar door.

"Manny, let me take the backpack."

He's glad to get rid of it.

We creep along, rubbing closer than the fog against that barn. What's left of the paint flakes off against my shoulder. There's this sweet scent coming from the cellar like from those gold things they swing around in church during slick, showtime Masses.

The chanting stops. We stop.

We creep around the far corner of the barn, facing the house. The front door is wide open, the fog sliding in and swirling around the front room. We creep up the front porch.

"Charley." I kneel in front of him. He stares at me kind of droopy-eyed. "I want you to sit here on the porch and watch the corner of that barn. You can do that, can't you?"

He nods.

"If anything comes around that corner, you ru . . . you move . . . as fast as you can into the house and tell us. I figure we can beat it out the back window. You can hop on my back, and we'll outrun it. No problem."

He sits on the edge of the porch, feet dangling, looking like a plaster angel set down there for decoration.

"Come on." I lug the blood through the front door like it's no big deal. Manny is close to breaking and I don't want to show him I'm freaked, too. The furniture in the living room is big and old. Not lumpy-and-stained old. This is see-yourself-in-the-wood, antique, *mucho dinero* old. There's fresh paint and varnish on the new stair rail and the hardwood. He must have paid a lot to have all this done, especially in such a short time. It's like a whole amazing world built from that crumbling shell.

"Hurry, let's get this over with," I snap.

"I can't do it," Manny says.

"Don't chicken out on me now."

"No. I *can't*." He waves a bottle at me. "It ain't coming out."

I take a bottle. Squeeze. Nothing. "Shit. It's gunky. Shake it."

Finally, a little oozes out. And then it's sort of squelching out in gooey threads.

Manny swirls his bottle in fast forward, waving it right where it'll squirt blood across a Persian rug that must be worth more than we'll see in our whole lives.

"What are you doing?" I hiss. "Squirt the wall."

I start on a wall, making the sign as small as I figure would be a passing grade to the Ace. I don't care how he'll find out we've done the job, only that he will.

I hear the footsteps on the porch. It's a klump-slide, klump-slide step, kind of like Charley's. Only it's something weighing a whole lot of Charleys.

I'm out the open back window, taking the screen with me. Manny is right behind. I'm halfway up the hill before it hits me that we ditched Charley. I stop, hands on knees, sucking air, Manny beside me.

"That old geeze, he's got Charley. Shit, Manny, how could I chicken out like that?"

Manny is too winded to answer.

"I'm going back for my brother. You go on home. You done enough." That's all he needs to haul ass. And I don't blame him.

I turn and walk back down the hill. The house is still dark. I sneak to a living room window and peek in. Charley lies curled up on the floor near the open front door. He looks dead. The old man sits on a chair, candlelight flickering across his face as he stares at my brother. He's the oldest guy I ever seen. The skin is tight and thin and crinkled so that you don't need X-rays to see his bones. I scope the claw hand. It really is a claw. Well, there are fingers and all, but they're twisted just like a claw. He makes a funny whistling sound when he breathes. He wears a dark suit and tie. He just sits there watching poor Charley like he's trying to decide, *baked or fried?*

Whatever this is, it's more than some cranky-old-man-kid story. Time to grow up. So I stand, walk to the back door, and knock.

He opens the door.

"My name is Richard J. Armante," I say in my in-your-face voice. "But guys just call me RJ."

"John Leguin," he says. "But you may call me Monsieur Leguin."

He steps aside just like I'm dropping by for a Sanka. I step in, trying to look like that's why I came, too. I'm making up a lame lie: *Hey, mister, has my runaway brother come this way?* Then that claw pinches my arm and leads me to a chair and I'm ready to spill my guts before the torture even gets to the part where he'll rip off my fingernails. He sits down across from me with his cane across his lap like a shotgun. Charley just lies there.

"Your sentry fell asleep on the job." He says it in a whispery whistle. "I believe you came back to save your brother."

"Yeah." I'm watching that blood drip down the wallpaper.

"That was a mistake," he says.

"Didn't have no choice," I say.

"Indeed." He presses the claws together in front of his lips, studying me real hard.

"How'd you know he was my brother?"

"Stands to reason." His eyes are watery, like the blue is melting into the white.

"What now?" An old-people funk comes off that chair even over the fresh smells, so I sit on the edge.

"As a matter of fact, I had been about to ask you the same question." The old man has an accent, like he speaks English too good for a normal person.

There's that whistling again. It's some kind of laugh. That makes me think of Mr. Sanders's snorting. I feel ashamed, just thinking of what Mr. Sanders would have thought about what I'd done tonight. But if I clean it up, to the Ace it'll be like I never done it.

"It's got to be scrubbed down," I say. "Then repainted, maybe. I won't work at night." Why am I saying this?

"Pull me up," he says.

"What?"

"Give me your hand. Pull me up."

I nearly puke as I reach out.

"Not my hand," he says. "Grab my wrist."

His hand grabs my wrist with hardly any squeeze, but there's some power, so I can't let go my grip. I pull him up real slow so that wrist won't snap. It feels like the old broom handles with chicken skin hanging from them that Manny and me made for our haunted house a long time ago.

"Arthritis," he says, still holding my wrist. "Tomorrow is not a school day?"

"Summer."

"That's fine. I will see you first thing."

Finally, he lets go.

CHAPTER SEVEN

CLAWS

I'm kneeling on the hardwood, scrubbing and scrubbing, as the afternoon sun glows on the last of the blood. Leguin sits in his chair, the cane across his lap, melting blue eyes studying me. The Blackjacks will know I undone the tagging. They'll make me pay as bad as if I never done it. I can't think on that now.

"So, Mr. RJ Armante," he says in that slick accent. "Does your mother know you're here?"

"I'm way past caring what my mom thinks. Sort of."

"Oh?"

"This is her day off, so she takes over the sibs. Lets me do what I want since I take care of them the rest of the time."

"Take care of them?"

"Yeah, you know. Cook, change, clean."

"Indeed." The way he presses his fingers together in front of his lips, it's like he's doing that church-and-steeple rhyme.

Why would an old man who looks near dead gather all his

stuff together and move to this lost valley? Into a broke-down farmhouse? In vampire movies, the creatures creep into a new village so they can find fresh blood to keep themselves alive. Well, the way Leguin is staring at me, I might be the fresh blood he's hunting.

I wrap the scrub brush and rags in the drop cloth, all the time pretending I'm not watching as he grabs the armrests and sort of twists out of that chair like it's a life-and-death thing.

I lug that gooey mess across the yard, feeling the old man staring at me from the porch. Finally, I'm around the back of the barn where he can't see me. I dump the drop cloth beside the incinerator and sneak over to the root cellar. The door is padlocked, and there's a red stain smeared against it. I walk back to the house like it's no big deal. Leguin sits on the porch steps staring at me, his cane hooked over the rail, a wine bottle and two glasses next to him.

"Well, all done," I say.

Leguin pats a spot on the steps, inviting me to sit, but I don't.

"Young man, you owe me an explanation as to why you smeared pig's blood in ungodly symbols across the walls of my home."

How do I explain the Blackjacks?

"There ain't no explaining what I did." I try and give him the in-your-face look, but it won't hold. I shrug. "It was just wrong. I'm sorry."

"Yes, and you have atoned for your sin," he says.

"Man, who are you to act like some priest hearing confession?"

"Who am I, indeed?"

I sit down on a lower step away from him.

"What are you waiting for?" He says. "Open the bottle. Pour the sherry."

It's cool the way he offers like it's no big deal. Maybe I'll just hang around for a sip. I pour us each a glass. Maybe Leguin is being what's called tactful, having us sit out here. With all the blood on my clothes, he don't want me sitting in that house.

"Cheers." He can hardly hold the glass with his twisted fingers. He's not so creepy in the sunlight, just a dried-up old man with a whole lot of pain eating away at him inside. But then, maybe it's like that Jekyll-and-Hyde thing.

I take a sip, ready for fire. But that stuff is sickening sweet, like syrup.

He makes weird slurping sounds and then turns to me. "You have strong PMA, young man."

"You would, too, if you'd been cleaning blood all day," I say.

There's that whistle laugh again. "PMA means positive mental attitude."

"Yeah? What's that supposed to mean?"

"A salesman must have a positive mental attitude in order to overcome the rejections."

"Sounds like more than just salesmen need it," I say.

"Indeed."

"So, you were some kind of salesman, then?" Nothing in the house or in what he says gives anything away about him, so I figure I'll sneak it out.

"I am . . . was . . . an insurance salesman."

"You? An insurance salesman? Get outta here."

"And you, no doubt, find the idea of selling to be vulgar."

"Don't know about this vulgar, but selling insurance sounds cool."

"Oh?"

"Yeah. Sort of living off your wits, if you know what I mean."

"Indeed." Leguin does that finger-steeple thing every time he says this.

"Yeah, I guess. What kind of insurance did you sell?" My clothes are stiff and sticky, and I'm mostly thinking about how to get out of here to get home and get them off and bury them for good.

"Life. I took great pride in that."

"Yeah?"

"Yes. You must believe in a product in order to sell it effectively." The old man hacks, and I wait for him to hock a loogie, but he's too polite. "Life insurance is the one form of insurance that is guaranteed to pay off." I'm not sure if he's laughing or coughing. Either way, it sounds like it'll kill him.

"That a joke?"

"Unfortunately, there is . . ." He sucks a couple deep breaths. ". . . there is one negative to being a life insurance salesman. One must inevitably dwell upon the morbid." The longer he talks, the more that weird accent sneaks in, kind of like that funky black-and-white Dracula.

"Morbid?"

"You, child, will make a fine life insurance salesman."

"Thanks . . ." I don't know what to say. It's not like being a fireman or an astronaut. "So, I suppose you learned about this PMA stuff from some book."

"Why do you sneer, child? You don't believe there's anything to be learned from books?"

"I didn't say that. I'm gonna write a book myself someday. Sort of a life story. Only I'll put in lots of made-up stuff, of course."

"Of course."

"And I wouldn't even feel bad about slipping in that made-up stuff, 'cause when it comes right down to it, made-up parts have the most for reals in them."

"Perhaps you would like to practice."

"What?"

"I would enjoy hearing one of these . . . tales. A childhood memoir, perhaps."

The way he says it, I can't figure if he's making fun of me or not. The sun is creeping down to the hills beyond the barn, darkening to Foxy Roxy purple. I've stayed too long.

"Indulge me." His eyes look like something you'd see peeking over a black cape, like he can hypnotize me.

I'm feeling a buzz from the wine. After what I done to his house, maybe I owe him one, and then I'll be free. Being here with this old man and all his fancy stuff, and having this whole house to himself, my story comes down to the Silverstream Rocket.

Then the story tumbles out and I'm just sitting there listening along, too. Like he reached his claws inside me and ripped out some plug.

The Tale of the Silverstream Rocket
and How I Toed the Line

So, there was this kid in my class at Our Lady's Grammar, Willy Schmidt, who was almost two years older than me 'cause his parents held him back a year so he'd be jumbo for football. I mean, he would've been the biggest kid even in the fifth grade, where he belonged. This one lunch he was jumping around in front of my face and yelling, "There was an old lady who lived in a shoe. She had so many children, she didn't know what to do!"

Well, it did sort of fit us. We live in a rounded, silver trailer with portholes like on a spaceship. It's called a Silverstream Rocket, and it's about the best trailer money can buy, even if ours is like a million years old. My mom sleeps in a room at the end of the trailer, like what would be the heel if it was a for real shoe. The sibs sleep at the other end like wannabe toes. There's this room built along the side that's even paneled and carpeted. I sleep there, being the man of the house, only I let Charley sleep there, too.

Anyway, that creep just kept repeating "Old Lady in the Shoe" like he was chanting Hail Marys. You know how a catchy tune can rattle around in your head over and over. And there ain't no escaping something in your head.

So that night after dinner, I put down the sibs and headed over to Mr. Sanders's trailer for advice. Mr. Sanders was the smartest drunk I'd ever known. He was the smartest anything I'd ever known. But no one else knew how smart he was 'cause no one else ever came near him. Once you got used to the smell, though, it was worth going there just for his stories. Like the one about this horny rooster. Or the one about this couple that do it up in a tree. Or this one about these dudes who kill each other for this gold under a tree. He had a lot of those Canterbury stories, which is an old book if you didn't know.

Mr. Sanders's trailer was on a concrete slab, not cinder blocks like ours. He had this sofa with the stuffing half gone that sat right out on the front of the slab like it was a patio. He was always sitting out there with Jack Daniels, his dog. He'd also have a bottle of the real thing. There was a sign on the side of the trailer over the sofa that he'd made that said YOURE HOOSTE. It wasn't even spelled wrong 'cause that was older English. It was supposed to mean "Your Host." I guess that was because he personally owned Canterbury Trailer Park all himself.

I sat on this beach chair he always got out 'specially for me. I told him all about that big fourth grader and the old lady who lived in the shoe. He just snorted, which was how he laughed. He said something like, "Sorry, but there is a humorous note to it."

I remember saying, "The humorous note is gonna be my fist in that creep's face."

"Violence is not always the answer," he said. Before he was a drunk, Mr. Sanders had worked with migrants for the government, something to do with housing. He'd even known that César Chávez guy. That's all got something to do with why he bought that old trailer park. I guess he planned for that place to be something special, like a human place for them to live. Of course, it never worked that way. Well, then he said, "We're all pilgrims. Even the bullies. All pilgrims."

So the next day at lunch that fourth-grade pilgrim was back in my face again. He just kept at it. "There was an old *lady who lived in a shoe. She had so many children, she didn't know what to do." There was like an echo behind him when a couple other guys repeated it. He just kept jumping around and around and singing it over and over. And pretty soon there were five, six, seven echoes laughing and repeating it behind him. That's when I figured it was time to do something about it right now or else it was gonna stick with me like forever.*

I got up real slick and rammed my fist up into his face. You gotta sock high when you go for the face 'cause you don't want to split no knuckles on teeth. I had to make that first punch last 'cause any extra punches were gonna be his. He just stood there with his mouth still going only no words coming out, like some big fish. Then the gusher poured out of his nose and he ran home.

I went back to class like it was no big deal. Everyone was just sitting real quiet while Father Speckler did that story about Daniel in the lion's den. They were all watching me and waiting for the summons from Mother Catherine.

And it came.

Mother Catherine was as big as any nun you'd ever wanna see. Man, she was bigger than any nun you'd ever wanna see. If you were lucky, she'd start in with this gurgle down in her throat, and that'd build into this foghorn yell that would rattle the wood-frame windows. She'd come so close she'd almost smother you with her chest. You were lucky if you got the foghorn, 'cause that meant she wasn't mad enough to give you no Thunder. She gave swats that rattled all the way up in your teeth.

You always knew Thunder was coming when she started talking to Sister Phyllis instead of you. Things like, "I can't

*imagine, Sister, what possessed this child to do such a thing."
That meant she was so POed she couldn't trust herself not to
take the Lord's name, or worse.*

*Sister Phyllis was like Mother Catherine's exact opposite.
She had this chirpy sparrow voice that she hardly ever used.
They were always together. Always. They even had this same
smell. They always smelled like maple syrup. Don't know
why. They just did.*

*"Sister Phyllis," Mother Catherine said, "once again this
young man is fast-breaking away from the Lord."*

*Then she turned to me and said the only thing she ever said
straight at a kid when she was so POed: "Toe the line, buster."*

*I didn't say nothing. I just put my toes on the red line painted
on the floor, and I bent over, grabbing the foot of Jesus on the
crucifix for balance. Jesus's feet were worn smooth from kids
grabbing hold. I stared under my armpit at her.*

*She just brought old Thunder straight back behind her ear,
swung level, never taking her eyes off the ball, so to speak,
with a follow-through that lifted me clear off my feet.*

She was batting a thousand for the Lord, like she said.

*It wasn't hard, not crying. I just aimed at the door and
started walking.*

"RJ."

I stopped at the door but didn't look back.

*"We love you, you know that." But it was Sister Phyllis
that said that.*

I just nodded.

*"Sure, he knows that, Sister. Now listen up," she said
straight at me. "You're playing with four fouls, buster. The
next one and you're out."*

Well, I should have paid her more attention.

CHAPTER EIGHT
FIGMENT

I'm marching home from Leguin's, hep-two-three, along
the river bottom. Cars and trucks are flying along the
freeway less than a mile away. But I'm in a whole other
world down here, thinking about today with the old man.
It's cool how he never butts into the tale, instead lets me
tell it to the end. If there is an end. It takes a good listener
to make a story whole, and he has a deep-down way of
listening.

A yellow moon floats behind raggedy old eucalyptus trees.
It's so dark in here, like that moonlight is being sucked up
by the mud that's supposed to be the Salinas. A couple more
weeks of dry and it won't even be mud, it'll just be all cracked
like that old man's face.

Then I see her. Even in that weird light, she looks like no
more than a darker shadow against the trees. Her back is to
me, and I can't see her purple toenails buried in the mud, but
I know it's Roxanne.

"Foxy . . . Roxy?" I try to say it sort of funny, but my voice cracks.

She turns and stares at me.

"It took you long enough," she says. "Jee-sus, is that blood? He hurt you?"

"It ain't nothing like that . . . What do you know about *he*?"

A sadness seeps up from way deep inside of her, like she's a part of that moonlight and the mud and the trees, and she don't answer me. Maybe it's not really her. Just a figment of my imagination.

"The Blackjacks are just up the road," she says.

"What do you know about them?"

"There's no escaping them."

"Come with me," I say. "We'll go back to the old man's and we can . . ."

"Listen to me. Don't you go back there. Ever. No matter what the Blackjacks might do. Don't go back to that cellar. Ever."

"Man, it was you that locked me in there in the first place."

"It ain't the same now."

Then she turns and climbs up the ravine, back the way I came. Back toward Leguin's. Like a figment lost in my imagination.

Guys used to play army down here, pow-powing and screaming and laughing. Then one day Roxanne had come charging down the bank, ambushing us like some enemy platoon. *How can you play these games*, she had screamed at me, *after what the war did to your own father?* The other boys had scattered and it had just been the two of us.

You don't know nothing, I had said. *My dad was a war hero and then he came home and he met my mom and they had me and then he died.*

"You don't know nothing," I say to the trees, feeling like I just been ambushed all over again. It's dark, but I know that river bottom, so it's no big deal. What would my dorky ten-year-old self think if he saw me coming at him all covered in this for real blood? He wouldn't even recognize me.

A song drifts out of the trees: *Time keeps on slippin', slippin' . . .*

I reach the bend and claw my way up the riverbank right smack into blinding headlights. Through my fingers I see two guys leaning against one of those old Chevy pickups with the big rounded fenders.

Blackjacks.

Wolfman's voice crackles out of the truck radio: *That's the Steve Miller Band, still on the charts.*

The Ace didn't send flunkies like Buns Bernie this time. Two big dudes with long greasy hair tied in bandanas. These are Jokers. Somewhere there's some kid safe in bed listening to that same station. I could dodge these creeps, but what's the point? They'd get me sooner or later.

"What's up?"

The Chevy is a primer gray that matches the taller guy's hair. Maybe they stole the truck and think if they repaint it no one will finger it.

"Get a load of this kid. What a mess." The gray-haired guy reaches in and punches off the radio, and then he lopes around me.

"I'd do a cherry red," I say. "With black pinstriping. Maybe some chrome running boards and tail pipes. Glass pack, for sure."

"Huh?" the other guy says. It hits me now that I've seen this guy from way back.

"This truck you stole. Maybe you don't want to bring attention on it. But no point stealing it if it ain't gonna be cherry. And don't you think sometimes the best disguise is right there in plain sight?"

It's his hair that threw me off. How does a twenty-year-old get gray hair?

"Hey, you're Brent Keating," I say.

"Shut up."

"You used to drive with your dad in his tow truck." Maybe if I can get him to see me, really see me, I might get out of this. "You came to our place a couple times to jump-start my mom's car."

"That piece-of-shit station wagon." I see by the twist of his face that I've just made things worse, maybe 'cause it reminds him that his dad is in prison now for jacking car parts.

"Get a load of all that pig's blood." The blond guy circles me in the opposite direction. I don't know him by name, but he's one of those older creeps I avoided in school.

"What were you doing at the old man's?" Brent asks.

"Cleaning up. He caught me."

"That's what the Ace figured." Their circle closes around me. "You didn't say nothing about the Blackjacks, did you?"

"No. He never asked."

"How can we be sure?" He thumps a fingernail against his teeth, pretending to think.

"I . . ."

"Shut up!" He slams me against the hood of the truck, needles shooting through my brain, my face against the warm metal. "Just listen. And don't screw up this time. Ace wants you to steal something from that old creep. Something valuable. One of those antiques he's got."

He slams me again, like that'll help me remember.

"Now pay close attention, just like your life depended on it. You're gonna steal something real valuable from that old man's house and you're gonna bring it to Camp Roberts. To those deserted barracks. Now for the good part. Just so you know we're serious."

Then they start pounding on me. Maybe it's this pain of each thud on flesh and bone that makes me forget, but they never say when. Never.

CHAPTER NINE

DOUBLE CROSS

I'm sitting on my sofa bed in the room that Charley's uncle built that runs the length of the trailer, staring through the screen at my sister Amy. She stands in the field behind Canterbury wearing her pleated uniform skirt even though school is out for the summer. Yellow ribbons tie her pigtails. The air reeks of baked dirt and dead weeds. She rocks on her heels with her hands behind her back as she watches her cat, Peabody, torturing some dying creature. It is Amy's favorite game.

That song drifts from somewhere across the trailer park and brings me back to the other night: *Time keeps on slippin',* *slippin', slippin' into the future . . .*

The Blackjacks have upped the game. But they never said *when* I have to deliver. This not knowing when, it's the worst. Charley bounces onto my couch, jolting my back. I can't hardly keep track of the days since the beating, but the deep, purpled pain that is now dulling into soreness is the truest measure of time. They could of done worse, but they want me around.

Slippin', slippin', slippin' . . .

Mr. Sanders, with his *Canterbury Tales*, he taught me about pilgrims that lived in a past that went back hundreds and hundreds of years. And Father Speckler, with his New Testament, he preached about a future that won't come until forever and ever, amen. Neither way does me any good now, against the Blackjacks. All I can do is live in my own here and now.

"Mom is gonna be mad for what you done with Stevieand-Suzy." That's about as long a speech as Charley ever makes.

He's right. Why do I do stupid stuff like I did with the twins today? I just get these ideas. What Mom calls bugs up my butt.

"Go check on Peanut and see if she's awake yet," I say.

I hear the engine of Mom's old station wagon, shuddering and turning over a couple times before it finally stops. She must be filling it with low octane, which means she is having trouble making ends meet again.

"I picked up the twins from practice." She's so big she blocks out the sun as she stands at the screen door. She folds her arms across her white waitress blouse, and her eyes drill through me. "You have anything to say for yourself?"

I stay seated with my left side away from her even though she's already seen the bruises. She made one big fuss, which is her way, and then dropped the subject unless I want to bring it up, which I don't. She's seen me with plenty of bruises before from fights or other stupid stuff. No way I want the Blackjacks and my family in the same world. No freaking way.

The twins peek from behind her. Suzy wears Stevie's

peewee baseball uniform, and it is dirty like it never is when he wears it. The cap hides her ponytail.

"How did 'Stevie' do?" I ask Suzy.

"*He* got a double," she says.

"Wow, his first hit of the season, and it's for extra bases."

Stevie smiles just as proud as if he'd made the hit himself.

"StevieandSuzy, go get out of those clothes." She turns to me: "Well, kiddo?"

"Stevie, he's been saying all along that he don't want to play. He hates hardball. I tried and tried to get him over it, but . . . And then there's Suzy. She wants more than anything to play hardball, but the coach won't let a girl on the team. And you, Mom, you're too busy to even notice."

She sits on the sofa, the springs groaning, and absentmindedly grabs for the big bead necklace that isn't there 'cause she can't wear it at work. If she starts chewing her hair like a little girl, then I'm home free. Instead, she brushes down her skirt with her big hands, draws a breath, and lets it out real slow.

"It don't change the fact you did wrong."

"Sorry."

"Well, I'll phone that coach tonight. He'll change his tune."

"It might help if you tell him it was Suzy who crushed that double. Stevie has struck out every at bat."

"Help, indeed," she mutters. "Go on, get out of here, kiddo. Go over to Manny's and have a good time."

I head out through the screen door, imagining the delicious smells coming from Abuelita's kitchen. But I won't be going to Manny's today. The Blackjacks expect me to steal something from that old man, and time is slipping. So I'm headed to Leguin's place for a double cross more dangerous than anything I pulled with the twins.

CHAPTER TEN
RIP-OFF

I'm making a lot of noise going up Leguin's front steps, not wanting surprises. It's almost dark. The lights are off, but the door is open.

"Mr. Leguin! Yo, Mr. Leguin!"

No answer. A breeze flaps the curtains. I walk in and pull the chain on a standing lamp with a fringy shade. Nothing. There's no bulb. I move from lamp to lamp. Nothing, nothing, nothing. That's just great. A candle in a silver candlestick that might be worth stealing sits on the coffee table, so I light that.

I know right away where he's hanging out. The root cellar. I don't feel like interrupting that, so I'm just wandering around, scoping the place out, checking for something I could rip off, something I could carry all the way to Camp Roberts and that the old man wouldn't notice right off was gone. I'm carrying that lighted candle, just like in those old horror movies, except the horror movies don't tell about that hot wax that oozes over your hand. Maybe I can be in and out with something before he even gets back.

The house is full of antique furniture, but none of it is rip-off size. Aunty Faith, who belongs to Amy, has so many family photos and ceramic cats in her apartment that I couldn't set lemonade down on a table without wiping out a whole row like dominoes. Old people are supposed to have all that stuff that stuck to them over the years. This old guy has nothing. Then, as I'm casing the joint, I see that the stuff don't look as big a deal as it did at first sight. Sofa cushions frayed. Wood armrests scratched. Silver chalice dented.

Funny I hadn't seen that the sliding doors to the dining room are closed. I walk over, still holding that candle, and slide the door open. It's dark like a cave. The candlelight flickers on old, dark wood against the walls. I take a couple steps into the room, aiming at the shadow of the dining table, except instead of a table it's a high old bed sitting right smack in the middle of the room. No problem. I can handle that. Now, a coffin, that'd be a problem. But a bed sort of makes sense. There's no way that old man's bones would make it up the steep old stairs to one of the bedrooms.

I should back out of here before he gets back.

I turn to make my escape when the candlelight bounces off a metal picture frame. The photo is all yellow and cracked inside that fancy silver frame. A bunch of soldiers sit staring at me. There's this one guy in the middle row on the right side, grinning like this is all a sick joke. Smooth Leguin's wrinkled skin, and it's his face in the picture.

"This is most disappointing." Leguin stands at the door, just outside the candlelight. "Most disappointing."

"I was just . . ."

"Yes. Quite." He turns and walks out of the room.

He's sitting in his chair when I come back out to the living room.

"Look, Mr. Leguin, I'm sorry. I was just . . ."

"Spare me your remorse. Light it."

"What?"

"Light it."

He nods at an old candelabra with a whole mess of candles that sits on the coffee table. The thing looks like it's for real silver. But it's just too big to carry off without him knowing. I'd have to creep back in the middle of the night when he's asleep. If he sleeps. I cup my candle so it won't blow out and begin to light the others.

"No."

"What?"

"Use that." He nods to a corner.

There's this long silver stick like the one I used to carry as an acolyte.

"You planning to perform some kinda Mass?" I ask.

He don't answer. I pick it up and light the wick. It takes forever to light all the candles.

"Fine. Only next time do it with more care."

What next time? I'm thinking.

"Pour us some sherry." His face looks red and waxy through that light.

I walk out to the kitchen and get the sherry and a couple of glasses. They're crystal. Definitely crystal. I could maybe bundle some glasses in my jacket, slip them outside the kitchen door, and come back later for them. Well, maybe I could. I'll think about it later. A box of Uncle Ben's rice and a banana peel lie on the counter. I check the fridge. About the biggest deal in there is a package of bologna. It's too depressing, so I head back to the living room.

"So, you got any jobs you want me to do?" I pour us the sherry.

"Sit."

I plop down in the overstuffed couch. We sit staring at each other. There's a smell from the old man's suit. It's the same smell as the plastic can behind the trailer where I kept Peanut's number-one diapers that needed washing.

"You forget to pay your electric bill?"

"I cannot abide artificial light." Not one wrinkle in that face even twitches.

"Right." If I had a mirror, I'd be checking it out for his reflection about now. More quiet. "You were in the army, huh?"

"That room and its contents are not open to discussion."

That kills the talk. I'm starting to feel warm from the sherry.

"Those appear to be serious bruises on your cheek and neck," he says.

"Them? I just got in a fight is all. No big."

"Another bully that you vanquished?"

I don't answer.

"Perhaps it is time for another tale," he says.

"I don't feel like telling no stories."

"Ah, but you have a gift for storytelling," he says, with that accent creeping in.

"Comes with practice," I say. "I can get so into a scary story that all the sibs end up curled together, their feet away from the edge of their beds so no tentacles or claws can snag their toes, lying there half the night just waiting for Mom to get home from work." I don't say out loud how telling a scary story in this place makes as much sense as Buns Bernie telling one of his dead baby jokes in a maternity ward. "Anyway, I don't feel like telling no scary stories."

My head feels a little dizzy from the sherry and it's getting too late to snag an antique. The Blackjacks are expecting a delivery, only God knows when. Maybe telling a tale will pass time until I can work out a plan to steal.

"Okay, here goes. One last time. I will call this The Tale of Father Speckler and . . . and My Spiritual Well-Being."

I should have thought ahead to how that story ends before I started in on it, but that's how life goes down.

The Tale of Father Speckler and My Spiritual Well-Being

Father Speckler, he was only supposed to be in charge of our spiritual well-being, like he said. He shouldn't have to worry about no temporal issues. But when they couldn't find no one to replace Sister Ellen after our fourth-grade class retired her, Father Speckler got stuck with us, like forever. He was a Jesuit, if you can believe it. Always going on about how he should be at some fancy high school like in King City. But no high school wanted Father Speckler and everyone knew it. He was hardly taller than a fourth grader, and he was bird skinny. It made the whole class scratch just watching him 'cause he never stopped moving. He was like those tiny birds that run away from the waves. He even called us that one time. Waves.

I don't even remember none of the things I did that got him so POed. He'd hop back and forth in front of us waves, and I just had to see how fast I could get him going. Sort of like an experiment. I'd mess up accidentally on purpose, and he'd hop faster. Then I'd just keep messing up and he'd just keep hopping.

But I'll never forget how it always ended. Sometime just after nutrition I'd say my last "Father," with an edge to it so he'd know I wouldn't ever want him to be my for real father. He couldn't punish me for words I was supposed to use. He'd stop. He'd even be shaking. Then he'd just open the door and point into that closet. So I'd step in and he'd slam the door behind me. I'd pull the chain on the overhead light and there'd be the lunches, all lined up on the shelf, the room full with the smell of peanut butter and bologna and mayo and Free-toes. Guys in the class hid comics in their coats so I could kick back on this chair I made out of some gray blankets that were put in there for emergencies like that and I'd just read and munch on Free-toes and Twinkies. It was as close as Our Lady's got to heaven.

Well, one day I said my one "Father" too many and he pointed to the closet. When I stepped in and pulled the chain, there was no light. He'd snagged the bulb. There was just this little crack of light from under the door. It had never been so hard to breathe in there before. All the lunches and even the blankets were gone. I just lay on that floor with my nose near the crack under the door listening to Father Speckler hopping back and forth. He was giving his little speech about how they were all God's children. Of course, me being in the closet, I was like Mother Catherine said, out of bounds to the Lord. The next day, Father Speckler even checked my pockets before sending me in there, and he snagged my M&M's and spare light bulb. My heart was pounding when that door clicked shut and it was even harder to breathe.

I knew there was no way I'd be able to live through no more closets. It was either me or Father Speckler. After lunch, he announced that there wouldn't be no more Bible Story Time. Instead, we'd have something called Science Project Demonstrations. Trust a Jesuit to bust Bible Story Time for something like Science Project Demonstrations. He picked me to go first. It was Friday, so I had the weekend to work on it.

I couldn't think of nothing, so Saturday night I headed over to Mr. Sanders's trailer. I sat in the beach chair and told him about the Science Project Demonstration. Mr. Sanders was quiet so I just listened to the hum of the CANTE BURY sign. He scratched Jack Daniels under the ear like he always did when he was thinking.

"Have you considered heredity?" he asked.

"Her what?"

"Heredity."

I said, "I guess I'd consider it if I knew anything about it."

He said, "Am I correct in assuming each of you has a different father?"

"Yeah," I said. "Except the twins. They got the same father."

Mr. Sanders started to say something, but stopped and just muttered something like, "Just forget it, RJ."

Of course, the more he warned me to forget it, the more my mind was working. I was thinking about my mom and the sibs and their fathers and finally my own father. And then, as I stared out at the CANTE BURY sign, I saw my Science Project Demonstration in that blue glow as clear as a saint's vision.

"But I'm done for tonight, Mr. Leguin. Maybe you'll hear the rest of the story another day. Then again, maybe you won't."

CHAPTER ELEVEN
STARDUST

I'm pedaling home from Leguin's on my dorky Stingray that's so small even my short legs bounce up to my chest. The chain is loose and I'm coasting as much as I can so it'll hold. Moonlight shines on the fields and on the foothills rising behind them.

What's wrong with me that I can't steal from that old man? It means I got to go back and try again. Or maybe it's not too late to sneak in after he's asleep and snag that silver candlestick. But he'd know right off I done it. I can't live with that. And if I go for another face-to-face, he's going to con me into finishing that story. I don't ever want to throw down the ending to the one I began today. Not the for real ending, anyway.

I turn the corner where the towering eucalyptus trees, planted for windbreaks, line the road. Beyond them runs the warped fence of the abandoned Stardust Drive-in. A glasspack muffler rumbles behind me. I look back. The car hasn't turned the corner yet, but I'm sure it belongs to a

Blackjack. I pedal past the crumbling Stardust sign and stare back at a familiar truck now turning the corner, and I veer off behind that broken galaxy. I toss the Stingray down in the overgrown weeds and scrunch behind the sign, shards of fallen stars digging into me. Keating's old Chevy truck with the big fenders is cruising slowly past. Even in the moonlight, the cherry red and the pinstriping and the chrome are kick-ass. Just like I said they would be. I feel a kind of power that I could turn a guy—a Joker—into making that truck what it should be, even if the stealing of it was wrong. Maybe I'm an accessory after the fact, like they say.

Don't the Blackjacks got anything better to do than follow some punk kid? If they catch me, they'll see I'm empty-handed and know I didn't take nothing. And then they'll decide I need another reminder. I don't feel like one of those, not on top of the bruises I already got.

"Look out, here come the police!" a DJ shouts from the truck's radio, a fake siren in the background. My heart jumps for a sec before that dude from the Police screams, *"Roxanne . . ."* and then the radio is twisted off in midscream.

"Enough of that shit," Keating says.

The Blackjack with the stringy blond hair tied with a bandana, the same dude from last time, laughs. "Freaky, the Police got a song about her, ain't it?"

"It ain't about her," Keating says. "Just the same name."

The truck drifts by, so I dig in behind the sign, peeking through the lattice. Keating is driving, and that greasy-haired Joker is next to him. And then there's Buns in the truck bed. It looks like his initiation is still going down.

"I lost my cherry in that drive-in. How 'bout you?" Keating says.

"Nah. I went for a darker place."

Listening to them, I think that evil might always be the same thing, but that it oozes out in different ways. The truck passes but stops at the corner. They know they've lost track of me. They turn right. That means they're going to circle the block and come back around.

When the truck is out of sight, I lift my bike up, ready to haul ass. The chain drops off and trails on the ground. No time to fix it. I should dump the bike and get the hell out of here. Instead, I grab it and sneak through the unhinged gate, past the tollbooth with its broken glass, and into the remains of the Stardust. I lean the Stingray against the fence beside the gate.

It has only been seven months since this place closed, but it is already a whole different world, alone and abandoned. The screen looms over me, reflecting moonlight. Panels have fallen, leaving gaps like crumbling teeth. The weedy asphalt, with its checkerboard of speaker posts, rolls down to a collapsed swing set on the playground at the base of the screen. When we were little, Mom would take us to the three-dollar-per-car show. We'd go play in our jammies on that shiny equipment below the towering screen. When we came back, Mom would have the station wagon backed up and the far back seat set up so it was facing the screen. Amy and me would sit there with Charley squeezed between us, waiting for that first cartoon.

There's the rumble of the truck coming around again. I check out the boarded-up cinder-block snack shack for a place to hide. Even if I find a way into it, I'll be trapped. The truck has stopped and is idling outside the entrance.

I dash for the back fence, where there might be an out.

"He's in there. I know it." Keating's voice.

"He needs another reminder," the other Joker says.

"Buns," Keating says, "get your fat ass out of there and check it out."

I find where we cut off the top of the fence boards to mark our spot, and I leap and grab the top of the wobbly fence and scissor my leg over until I'm riding the top. Then I stand, balancing myself, the loose boards shaking, and leap to a limb of a tree beyond the Stardust. From there, it's an easy climb up a few branches to our platform.

"See anything?" Keating calls.

Buns has his back to me, staring up at the screen, and don't answer.

The floorboards shimmy as I lie down and peek through the branches, sniffing that cough-medicine scent of eucalyptus.

I can see Buns walking around, looking for me. His jaw is open like he, too, is overwhelmed by the sadness.

Manny, me, and this kid called Dud built this platform just beyond the fence so we could watch the movies for free. Of course, we could have watched them for free down below, by just jumping the fence and then spending the night running from any snack shack guys they sent out to catch us. For the boring movies, that was more fun than watching. But for more real movies, up here was the place. Fridays we'd fall asleep to the sounds of *Star Wars* lightsabers humming and then wake up at dawn and sneak home.

Buns is wandering toward the fence. Does he know about this platform? A few guys had found out. Was he one of them? Can't remember.

Now the Jokers come into the drive-in and join Buns. Looking at him next to these Blackjacks, it don't seem possible I was ever afraid of him. I can sense he's having second thoughts about joining, and I almost feel sorry for him. Almost.

"Well, you see him?" Keating runs his hand through his long, gray hair.

Then Buns turns and glances up into the trees straight at me. The blond dude follows his stare, but Buns looks away and shrugs.

"Nah," Buns says. "He probably jumped the fence and ran home."

"No, he didn't. Look here." It's the blond-haired guy. "The kid's bike. The chain's undone. He wouldn't leave his bike. He's probably hiding, waiting until we leave and he can get it."

"Hey, kid!" Keating calls. "We know you're here."

Like I'm gonna answer. Will Buns tell them?

"Check the snack shack, fatty," the blond says.

Buns wanders over to it.

"RJ won't go in there," Keating says. "He knows he'd be trapped."

Keating cups his hands and shouts: "I know you're out there! The Ace says you got one week and a day. One week and a day. Noon. You already know where."

Well, that is more time than I hoped, but less than I need. No more slippin'.

"We're taking your bike!" the other Blackjack shouts.

"No, we ain't," Keating says.

"The hell. My nephew could use this."

"Leave it," Keating says.

"You ain't the Ace."

"I got the truck. I say we leave it."

"You're getting soft."

"Not hardly. But I'm the only one with the brains here. If RJ can't get around, then he can't do his delivery." Keating turns and heads back to the entrance and the other two have to follow if they want his ride. "If he can't do his delivery . . ." Keating is shouting like he's talking more to me than to them. ". . . then the Ace is out something more valuable than this sorry bike." Truck doors slam. "And if he ain't happy . . ."

The roar of the truck drowns out the rest. I wait until I hear the truck rumble away, in case they're trying to trick me. But after they're gone, the wait stretches into something else as I don't want to come down.

It was *Saturday Night Fever* that killed the Stardust.

We were pumped when we saw the movie trailer announcing it was the next show after *Star Wars*. Not that we really cared about the story. It looked lame and we'd rather lie out there every Friday night forever falling asleep to *Star Wars*. No movie replacing that stood a chance. But *Saturday Night Fever* had one thing *Star Wars* didn't. It was rated R. And not R for violence. This was R for sexual content and nudity. The Stardust had never shown one of those before.

At first, if I ignored the music, *Fever* wasn't so bad. But there was no nudity through most of it. Still, the part about the gang was cool. And I liked the older brother when he quit the priesthood. But then there was this girl, Annette, who was all messed up and reminded me of Roxanne. She even looked like if Roxanne cleaned herself up. Then, by halfway through, I was thinking that if this was what love was supposed to be, I didn't know why anyone bothered. And by the time it got to that bridge scene, and what those guys did to Annette, I was done with that movie and wished I could unwatch what I just seen, but there was no chance of that . . .

It's a yipping sound that wakes me up. I stare over the side of the platform and spot three coyotes slinking between the speaker posts. The summer drought has driven them from the hills. I could jump down outside the fence and go home without facing them, but the bike is still inside and I'm not going to leave it. I should wait until they leave, but I'm done waiting and I'm done hiding. So I crawl down to the top of the fence and then jump inside the Stardust. The coyotes freeze. The biggest one is in front of me and the other two are spread out on either side.

The hell with this. I wave my hands in the air, scream, and run right at that mangy thing. "Aaawwwwwww!!!" And damn it if he don't turn tail and run, the other two joining him. I chase those yipping cowards clear out the entrance.

Then I return to the Stingray and kneel and dig the chain out of the weeds.

I could make one last attempt at stealing from Leguin. But I know it's no good. I can't do it. I need another plan.

The chain is gunked with grease and dirt and weeds.

Maybe I can go to Mrs. Elliot's Antiques and Collectibles Emporium and buy something that looks fancy but don't really cost a lot. Something I could pass off as Leguin's.

I take the knife out of my back pocket and flick it open and pry it between the chain and the sprocket, carefully working one notch at a time.

I got a few bucks stashed I could pay her, but that won't be enough. Damn, that means I got to come up with some quick con to make a few bucks. But it don't make sense stealing from one place to avoid stealing from another. Father Speckler called that stealing from Peter to pay Paul. Or something like that.

The chain catches and I lift the back tire and spin it. Not great. But it will hold. I hop on and cruise past the ticket gate, and it's *adios* to the old Stardust. The chain slips once as I turn onto the street, but then catches again. The Blackjacks are gone. Just me alone.

There is another way to get cash. I haven't done it in years, and it won't be so easy as back then. And even in those days, it could get tricky. Still, it might work. Only problem is that it's sort of like stealing from God. But I'm counting on Him forgiving me for a whole lot worse than stealing before I die, so why not?

CHAPTER TWELVE
CONFIRMATION

I'm sitting in the shadows in a corner of the chapel at Mission San Miguel Arcangel, waiting for the right tourist prospect to wander in so I can make that cash. The mission sits outside Arcangel Valley, but it's about as close as tourists get to wandering into our little world. I used to be a sort of unofficial tour guide here. I made more than a few bucks off tips. But that was when I was eleven and being cute was still a factor. Now the best I got to work with is obnoxious.

The summer heat pounds outside, but it feels sweet soaking in this cool air and listening to my breath sliding across adobe walls. It smells like two hundred years of prayers seeping out of the oak pews as I squirm down, waiting for a prospect. No matter how many times I look, I always see something new on the walls, what they call frescoes. The high walls all crammed with designs painted in greens and blues and golds like someone went crazy with funky wallpapers, these big pictures on the side walls that could be fans or seashells depending on your mood, a wall pulpit painted in blues and greens and reds and yellows and even some gold and silver, the altar surrounded by for real pink pillars and all kinds of tiles with squiggly shapes, and above that altar this all-seeing eye of God in its triangle, sitting in a cloud, with these 3-D sun rays bursting out of it. How do you figure something that trippy in a for real church? A product of divine madness, Father Speckler had called it.

How does a kid kneel and take God with that eye staring down at him?

The door creaks open, and I scrunch down in a pew. Newlyweds, hands glued together, creep into the chapel. We get a lot of newlyweds passing through on their way to the Madonna Inn. I wait until they start gawking around before I make my move. I don't want to interrupt if they pray. This couple moves to the altar and stares up at that all-seeing eye. I sneak down the aisle toward them.

"You know there's bones buried right under that altar?" My voice cracks, and I wish for that choirboy alto that used to make ladies smile. The couple stare at me. "Father Martin is buried right under that altar. Died in 1824, so I bet there's only his bones by now."

"Yes, the pamphlet mentioned him," the guy says as the two of them edge away.

"That's the wishing chair you're heading to over there. It's like magic. Girls are supposed to sit in it and get their wish, like about love. I ain't kidding. You can check the pamphlet. It's all there."

He does check the pamphlet, and his face comes up looking impressed when he finds it's for real.

"Esteban Munras did all this in 1821." I wave at the walls.

"They're frescoes. He trained Indians to do it. Fun fact: more than a hundred thousand Indians died building the missions. Moving on."

I nudge them out to the grounds. Even in the shade of the archway the heat pounds at us.

"There was this one priest, Father Antonio de la Concepcion Horra. Now, there was one weird dude. Got freaked out about the ants. Kid you not. Maybe there were 'untold millons' like your pamphlet says. Or maybe he only thought there were. But they for sure got on that guy's nerves. He did all kinds of weird things to get rid of the ants, even shooting off guns to try and scare them away, which worked better on the Indians than it did on the ants. He went totally bonkers and got hauled back to Mexico in chains."

"I understand there's a cemetery." The wife's question nearly throws me off my game 'cause it's usually just old people that want to check out the cemetery, sort of shopping around maybe.

"You sick?" She does look sort of pale.

"Sick? Eh, no, why?"

I shrug.

The man looks up at the sky like for spiritual help. I feel my tip melting away in this heat, so I herd them through the courtyard toward the convent living room. The Reeds make for a tight closer.

"In the 1840s, the mission couldn't make it no more, and so this scumbag Pío Pico sold the mission to the Reed family for six hundred bucks, and so it wasn't a mission no more. Well, Reed went off during the gold rush, and wouldn't you know he struck it rich and came back with a pile of gold dust. You can figure gold never leads to no good. These deserters from an English warship stopped here. The Reeds were all nice to them and gave them food and shelter. But this Mr. Reed, he started bragging about that gold. Well, those men thanked the Reeds for being so nice and stuff and they left. I think they spent the night up in this canyon, where there's this big oak tree now. It's sort of a haunted place, but you won't find that in no books. Anyway, they came back at night. They didn't just steal the gold. They murdered the whole family. Women, children, servants . . . eleven people! They just dumped their bodies in this here convent living room right where you're standing now."

The lady grabs her husband's arm. Like I planned it, they are happy to follow me out into the light of that parking lot.

"A posse like out of some Western trapped those killers on some cliffs. Shot one guy. Another one jumped and smashed his guts on the rocks. The other three were hanged. They never found the gold. I think it might be buried up in that canyon."

Finally, the lady gives the guy a nod. Each couple uses a different signal, but it always means the same thing. *Let's dump this kid and get back to the Madonna Inn and that caveman room.*

I have them climbing into their car and five bucks sliding into my pocket. I head back into the chapel for one more troll. As I wiggle back down in the cool dark corner and wait, I can almost hear my sweet solo recessional filling that chapel during that slick showtime confirmation, with the girls in their stiff white dresses and the boys squirming in their coats and ties. That was the last time I sang choir 'cause then my mom told me about my dad having my same sweet voice.

A girl creeps into the chapel. With that straight oil-slick black hair and milk-glass white skin, I know right off it's Roxanne, except that I haven't ever heard of her being in church. She wears a white sheet that's been sewed into a raggedy dress, these big red stitches tying it together just under where her tits bump out, and red ribbons stitched along the sleeves and a red sash around her waist.

Roxanne peeks around, and I slide down in the pew. She's whispering a song, and I hear "Roxanne" and then the part about a red dress, and I know it's that new Police song, and that Roxanne is just crazy enough to think it was written about her.

Then she glides down the aisle like some kind of wannabe bride. At the altar, she glances around like she don't know what to do next. She sees the wishing chair and walks over and sits down in it, closing her eyes. Her chewing gum *click-click*s like pebbles plinking against the adobe. Roxanne isn't your tourist prospect, but she looks in bad need of a guide right now and there's no one around except me.

She opens her eyes when she hears my steps, but she don't move.

"That's a wishing chair," I whisper when I reach the altar.

"Don't you think I know that?" she says.

The quiet hangs on so long I can't hardly stand it.

"Didn't know you were Catholic," I say.

"I ain't nothing."

"I don't get it."

"I just want to be confirmed."

"But if you're not . . ."

"You know, *confirmed*."

She looks at me like I'm a total dork.

Staring into a face that's half hate and half sad, who am I to tell her she's mixed up on this confirmation stuff?

"I should've known I wouldn't find it here," she says. "I like this place, though. Hey, you used to be in that children's choir. I heard you even had solos."

"I don't sing no more."

"Did I ask you to sing?"

She hasn't said about our meeting by the river, which makes me think it really was a figment.

"Confirm me."

I don't know if she says this, or if it's just the wind snickering off adobe walls.

"What?"

"Confirm me. You ain't much, but at least you know what to do."

Is she really expecting me to be a wannabe priest? It sounds like a sin, but I can't figure it for sure. That all-seeing eye stares down at me.

"You know what a priest says or does, don't you?"

"Sort of, but . . ."

"Well?"

"I ain't a priest."

"Duh. That don't matter to me."

I can tell myself it's only playacting at being a priest. Except that Roxanne, whatever she wants, it isn't playacting.

"Okay, well the priest, or a bishop if it's big-time, he presses the sign of the cross on your forehead with his thumb."

"That's it?"

The way she asks makes the whole thing sound so cheap. Except that when I look into those black eyes I see there's nothing worth more to her than being confirmed.

"I don't know if this is for real," I say, "but I heard that in the good old days the bishop would slap you. Man, I'll bet he'd knock that Holy Spirit right into you." I wait for her to laugh. I never understood that part myself. But Roxanne just nods like she knew all along that being confirmed had something to do with someone hitting you.

"Okay, slap away." She squeezes her eyelids shut like she's done this part before.

"It's not like that no more."

She just sits there, eyes squeezed shut, in that sorry white dress stitched in red. I edge around so I can't glimpse that all-seeing eye, only I still feel it through the hairs on the back of my neck.

"Go on."

I check out the pews to make sure no novitiates are lurking around, and I lift my hand clear to my ear like Mother Catherine when she's swatting me with old Thunder. But I can't. I just reach out and touch her face.

"That ain't a slap." She opens her eyes.

"I can't."

"Ain't nothing easier than a slap."

"I can't."

"You don't do it and I won't be confirmed."

I pull back my hand. She scrunches her eyelids closed.

"Receive the Holy Spirit."

My hand smacks her cheek.

"That it?" She stares at me for just one sec, but in that sec I feel closer than I ever felt to anyone.

"Yeah, that's it."

"Ain't there something else?"

"I already said I don't do songs."

"Well, at least we gave it a try, huh?" Her eyes slide back to cold and faraway.

"What'd you expect? I ain't a priest."

She wanders back down the aisle toward the door. *Jesus loves the little children* slides up my gut . . . *all the children of the world* . . . and I squeeze my insides, feeling that song twisting through me, sliding like sickening sweet incense up my throat. I clench my teeth together and keep that song all bottled up inside me.

Roxanne takes the gum from her mouth and sticks it under the last pew. Then, without looking back, she disappears into that heat like she's being sucked up into the light.

CHAPTER THIRTEEN

BUYING TIME

I'm standing next to Charley, fingering a wad of crumpled bills in my pocket and looking up at the homemade sign propped against the chimney on the roof of the old clapboard house:

MRS. ELLIOT'S ANTIQUES AND COLLECTIBLES EMPORIUM

Drivers can see that sign clear over on 101. There's another sign hanging from the porch:

A TURNE OF THE CENTURY HISTORICAL
FARMHOUSE AND MUSEUM
TOUR: 50C

Mrs. Elliot gives prospects the so-called tour for free to make them feel good and then tries to sell them some of her stuff that's been in her family a million years, complete with its family history. Only she's so attached to most of the stuff that she mostly changes her mind and won't sell it and the prospects either stomp out all POed or scratching their heads like they don't know what the hell is going on.

Charley starts right away limping for the back gate. Mrs. Elliot's backyard is the unofficial junkyard in town, filled with what she calls the collectibles.

"Not today," I say. "Today, we're going inside."

Charley looks impressed. We've never bought inside before, but if I'm to pass off something to the Blackjacks that I pretended I stole from Leguin, then it's got to be primo.

Mrs. Elliot has all of six prospects wandering around inside, which is the major rush before the Fourth. She's dressed for the crowd in her baby-blue square-dance outfit. There are all these frilly underskirts that make it look like she's being felt up by a gang of butterflies, but she do-si-dos through that room without even wiping out a chamber pot.

I just sort of browse, not wanting to disturb her in action. Charley bangs against a hat rack, which I grab before it smashes across a table covered with little colored glass bottles.

"I knew I shouldn't of let you in here," I whisper.

The prospects check us out like we're part of the emporium—the weird local and his crip brother.

There's an old clock that looks like it could be from Leguin's mantel. It even keeps good time.

"Moving your business inside, RJ?"

I jump at her voice. Don't know how I could've missed the *swush* of her skirts.

"Just looking," I say.

"You been looking a long time." Mrs. Elliot's chins wobble under her lizard lips, making a scratchy sound on the frilly neckline.

"Where's Charley?"

"In the kitchen with some cookies," she says.

I point at the clock. "It don't even chime."

"But it keeps perfect time," she says.

"Don't suppose it's all that old," I say.

"Antique," she says.

"Well, then it's too old."

"Depends on how you look at it."

"So how much?"

"A funny thing about that clock."

Here comes the family tale. I'm in no mood for a story, but it'll drive up the price if I look rushed. And her stories are pretty good, the way she mixes the for real and make-believe until even she can't tell them apart.

"A sad story." Her neck wobbles against the lace as she closes her eyes and shakes her head. This is laying it on pretty thick, even for her. "Do you know the young lady . . . she must be about your age . . . no, a little older . . . thick dark hair . . . her grandfather was a Martin from over in Gonzaga. They all have that kind of hair. Mission Indian. Anyways, you must know the child. Mrs. Elston says the girl's mother used to lock her up in the house. Everyone was afraid to say anything because of her mother's boyfriend, who works at that new uppity winery they built near Santa Maria . . ."

"You mean Roxanne?" So this isn't a family story after all.

"Yes, Roxanne is her name."

"Well, what about her?"

"Oh. Well, it seems she has disappeared."

"Disappeared?"

"Just like that. Vanished into thin air. A regular mystery.

Of course, everyone assumes she ran away. But if you ask me, something is not right. It was just terrible the way her mother and that boyfriend treated the girl. Why, they could have done something bad to her. Or she could have done something to herself, the poor child."

I just want to be confirmed . . .

"Are you sick, RJ?"

"I'm . . . I'm okay." It's only a day less than a week since she slipped out of that chapel. Man, news flies fast around this valley, like there's no time at all. "But what does she got to do with this clock?"

"I bought it from *her*. That must've been right before she disappeared. You know, I suspect it may be stolen."

"Why do you say that?"

"I knew that poor white-trash mother of hers didn't have anything fine like this. So I asked the girl. I said, 'Where did you get such a lovely timepiece?' 'Oh, it's not mine,' the girl said. 'It belongs to that old man living at the Miller farm.'"

"Mr. Leguin," I say.

"Yes, I believe that's the man. Do you suppose he is really moving in there permanently? Who would do that? Well, she said she was selling it on his behalf."

What does Leguin have to do with this? Why would he even need more money? Could he somehow be responsible for her disappearance? Had he given her the clock, or had she stolen it? What was it she'd said down by the river . . . *Don't go back to that cellar. Ever.* Maybe she hadn't been a figment after all. Maybe she had been on her way to do what I couldn't.

"RJ, please, sit down. You look ill."

"No, I'm okay." If it really did come from Leguin's, then

it would be all the easier to pass off. Hell, it wouldn't even be passing it off. "So how much for the clock?"

"Forty-five dollars." She don't look straight at me 'cause we both know it's worth a lot more than that and she's trying to do some kind of charity act, which if she is I won't go for it. Still, I should lowball her offer just out of principle.

"Okay, I'll take it."

"Sold, then."

You'd think my face was a mound of zits the ways she's checking it out, wondering why the hell I want this clock. I can just see her adding me to the mystery of Roxanne and the clock. She'll be telling the next prospect about the little trailer-trash boy living with all those brothers and sisters—all from different fathers, you know—and how can he afford that clock and what is he going to do with it?

She picks up the clock and walks out to the kitchen to close the deal. Charley has finished a whole tin of cookies. Mrs. Elliot bends over and pulls a pencil stub out of her white sock. She wears high-toppers with thick athletic socks, which don't exactly go with the skirts. But she has corns. She squishes her nose up against the wall as she scribbles 45 on my tab, added right on the wallpaper next to the back door.

"No, I'm paying cash."

"My goodness."

I count the bills into her hand. "You have something I can cover the clock with?"

She grabs a large towel off the refrigerator door handle and hands it to me.

"Thanks." I wrap the clock in the towel and go out the back door.

Charley walks on account of I'm lugging the clock. He can

keep up with me at this speed since we're going by way of the alleys and I'm creeping along so as not to mess up the mechanics in the clock. What kind of chump prospect am I that I buy something with cold cash and then pretend I stole it?

"RJ, why are you laughing? You're scaring me."

"Buying time, Charley. That's all I'm doing, buying time."

He don't even ask what that means, which if he did I wouldn't tell him anyway. He just stares at me the whole time I laugh.

CHAPTER FOURTEEN

MUUMUU

I'm lying with my head against the arm of the sofa, staring at a June bug bumbling against the screen. It's so typical of this place that the June bugs don't bother to show until July. The clock lurks inside the backpack under the sofa, waiting for tomorrow's delivery. This used to be my all-time most favorite time, the long afternoons with the sun taking forever to drop below the hills. The Garcias three trailers over are talking softly, but I hear each word. Someone is firing up a barbecue, and I inhale the scent.

I smell the warm cloth from my mom ironing inside the trailer and hear that *ku-swuussh* from the iron. That sound used to make me feel warm inside, but now that I've grown away from her, it just makes me feel lonely. Her big plastic beads click like a rosary as she presses other people's clothes.

"Hey, kiddo!" she calls.

I don't answer.

The *ku-swuussh* turns into a hiss, and I know she's put down the iron. The door opens and she steps down to the porch. She's wearing her lime-green muumuu covered by strands of brightly colored beads.

"Hey, kiddo, this is your mother speaking."

She fills the whole room when she walks across to my couch bed. Everything about her is big and bright and cheerful. Sometimes I hate her for not giving me none of her bigness.

"What is it, Mom?" I just keep staring out the screen.

"'What is it'? Well, for starters you could come down to planet Earth."

"What's that supposed to mean?"

"I mean the way you been behaving this summer. You got a little girlfriend, don't you?"

"What?"

"Yeah, that's it. The way you're moping around and disappearing at all hours. You got yourself a little girlfriend." She laughs with that deep chuckle, sending the beads all clicking at once. It used to be she'd start that laugh and I couldn't help but laugh with her. That's how she always got me out of funks, as she calls them. Laughing is the best medicine, she'd say. But this time I'm not laughing. "Hey, Earth to kiddo. So what's her name? Anyone I know? I'll bet it's that little Martinez girl, Theresa."

She sits on the couch and it sags and I wonder if she'll squish the clock.

Sometimes she just nails me dead-on, like about how I like Theresa, and it makes me so mad. I got no secrets, not even way deep inside. Well, she might think she knows everything, but I won't ever let her know about the Blackjacks, no matter what. Serves her right. And then the words just come out.

One of those just-for-the-hell-of-it lies a guy says when he's all POed: "It's Roxanne. We got a thing going."

Just as fast as my words, her hand flashes out and slaps me, the healing bruises burning deep into my cheek. It's only the second time she's ever hit me.

There's a long quiet with just the bumble of that stupid June bug.

"Don't you ever say that. You can't have nothing to do with her. Nothing. Tell me you were joking."

"Okay, so I was kidding." I don't give her the satisfaction of seeing me rub my cheek. "You don't got to worry about Roxanne, anyway. She's gone. At least, that's what Mrs. Elliot told me."

"Mrs. Elliot told you that? She may be a busybody, but she's usually right. It don't surprise me, the way that girl was treated at home."

"Why do you hate them so much? I hardly ever heard you say bad against anyone except Roxanne's mom."

"Well, it's past time you heard this, I suppose." She clicks the beads one at a time through her thick fingers. "Your father had been engaged to Roxanne's mother . . . Helen, you know . . . when he went into the army and then disappeared overseas. Then she took up with another man while he was gone. We were both waitresses at Dan's. Lord, what a scene that was when your father stomped in, Helen's new boyfriend sipping coffee at the counter and flirting with her. The war in Vietnam hadn't started yet. At least not that one we were to know about. But your father, he was over there in Southeast Asia. He came back changed. Not the gentle boy we all remembered. He beat into that guy . . . You could hardly even call it a fight. Helen lost her job over it. Your father spent time in jail. I visited him and we sort of fell in love during that first long talk. Helen's boyfriend was gone before your father even made bail. After that, she thought she could get her clutches back into your father." Mom snorts like that was the craziest idea anyone ever had. "Well, there you have it. The short version, anyway."

Man, never trust a short version of a tale.

She pats my knee, lifts herself from the cushions, and steps back into the trailer.

I picture Roxanne standing in that riverbed, maybe just a figment . . . I see her walking out of that chapel into the heat . . . and my brain says, *Sure she ran away.* But deep down in my heart I feel that she hasn't left. Something about that girl with the red stitches, who wanted to be confirmed, tells me she wasn't ready to run away. But if she hasn't run away, where could she be? Mrs. Elliot thought maybe her mom or that boyfriend could have done something to her. But her mom was more into the deep-down-inside kind of hurt, not the physical.

Maybe she's hiding out with some boy, or shacked up with some older guy. But if she's doing that, she wouldn't hide it. More like she'd flaunt it, rub it in her mother's face. What if she done something to herself? The more I think on it, the more likely that sounds . . . But she wouldn't do that in secret, either.

Then again, what did she have to do with Leguin? *Don't you go back there,* she warned me. Maybe she's trapped in that root cellar and that's why it's locked. Or maybe even he's killed her and her body is locked in there. He wouldn't do that . . . would he?

Well, why should I care? She's nothing to me. Worse than

nothing the way she picked on me all these years. I got my own problems to think about. Tomorrow morning I'll haul this old clock clear to Camp Roberts and hope it's enough to buy off the Blackjacks.

Why should I care about her?

CHAPTER FIFTEEN

THE KILLING TREE

Manny is sitting at the big table waiting for me when I come up the back steps onto the porch. The summer sun has made his skin almost as dark as our faded black tees.

"This sucker is heavy." I don't bother with a saber-swoosh as I drop the backpack, the clock *clunk-gong*ing, and grab the styrofoam coffee cup Manny holds out to me. Everything is throwaway at Manny's house. Abuelita stares at me from the kitchen, shakes her head, and turns away.

"That sounds like a clock . . . You delivering an old clock?" His voice edges up into fear. "What if it breaks?"

"Yeah, it's an antique clock," I whisper. "You think the Blackjacks would settle for less? It's gonna be a hell of a walk to Camp Roberts. You don't have to come, you know."

Manny's answer is to stand, cross his arms across his chest, and stare at the bruises yellowing under my freckles.

"Nino-'n-Smitty are taking some workers out past King

City." His voice is low and quiet again. "They'll be driving right by it."

"Will they take us?"

Manny shrugs. Pickers wander out of the garage, their faces shadowed by cowboy or baseball hats, bandanas around their necks, joking to each other. I catch a lot of their words, but not enough to understand their stories. A wrinkled old guy is helped up onto the truck bed by a kid young enough that he could be hanging out with Manny and me.

"Hurry!" Manny says.

I grab the backpack. By the time I reach the truck, Nino-'n-Smitty are already loading the last of the workers in the back.

"Can you drop us by Camp Roberts?" Manny calls.

"You thinking of enlisting?" Smitty laughs.

Nino holds my chin with his thick hands and checks out the bruises on my face.

"Been in a fight, *mijo*?"

"Can we go?" I ask.

Even though I'm waiting for them to say okay, I'm hoping they'll ask why. If they just say that one word . . . "why" . . . then this whole creepy mess will spill out of me and it will be in the hands of grown-ups I trust, and so I won't have to carry the worry no more. Nino lets go my face and tugs on the ends of his mustache and Smitty combs his fingers through that stringy beard, just thinking it over.

"Okay, *hombres*. You can sit on the tailgate." Nino grins. "If you can hang on."

Nino-'n-Smitty walk around to the cab.

Well, who am I, thinking some grown-ups can fix my problem? I'm RJ and I'm fifteen and I can do this. Then, just maybe, the Blackjacks will leave me alone and I will have done it myself, with some help from Manny.

Those pickers just stare at us as I lift the bag onto the edge of the truck bed. The truck edges forward, and we run after it and jump, grabbing the side gates so we don't fall out, our feet dangling over the edge.

The truck grinds down the driveway as I get a last peek of the killing tree and that empty tub. Of course the Dead blasts from the 8-track: *Trouble ahead, trouble behind, and you know that notion just crossed my mind.* There's no shocks left on this thing, so every time we hit a bump, I clutch the clock and almost bounce off the back. We head out onto the frontage road. There's not a cloud in that white-blue sky. Nowhere for a heaven to hide in a sky like that. It hits me for the first time ever that someday I won't be around to see any more skies. I hope that someday is a long way off, but who really knows?

"Manny, do you believe like in heaven and all that?"

He looks at me funny. "Go to Mass, don't I?"

"That proves nothing." I hold on to the bag as we hit a bump and there's a *gong-clunk.* "I mean, it's like the guys Mrs. Harper called the Immortals that she had hanging in class."

"Shakespeare and them guys," Manny says.

"Yeah. And they weren't even saints or nothing. Just regular guys that got to live forever on account of other guys are still reading their books."

"So?"

"So that ain't right," I say.

"So?" Manny just stares at me with a scowl on his face. He don't like guys to mess with his religion.

"So, I'll give you ten to one that if you went and found that Shakespeare's coffin and you ripped the lid or whatever off, you'd just find a pile of bones with this skull to one side sort of grinning up at you and a couple pieces of hair maybe still hanging on and maybe a part of his coat wrapped around the bones."

"Immortal has to do with your soul, like you didn't know."

The truck crawls uphill. The tailpipes are right below us and we're sucking up black exhaust. Then we're going downhill and the black exhaust is gone and the road is racing under our feet.

"Okay, then suppose Shakespeare's *soul* is like up on a cloud somewhere watching people read his books. Makes you wanna make sure a writer is still alive before you flip his pages, so you don't got some ghost reading over your shoulder."

Manny don't answer, just turns away. It's my fault for bringing up this immortal stuff. He feels bad about his mom, but that's just water under a bridge. What if my dad is on a cloud watching me? I've never done him proud. Maybe never will.

The truck shudders to a stop at the edge of Camp Roberts, and we hop out. Since the war ended, chunks of the base have been abandoned. I grab the bag and Manny pounds the side of the truck and it grinds down the road. The migrants stare back at us like we're the ones hanging from that killing tree.

CHAPTER SIXTEEN

BIXBY

We cross the frontage road to the chain-link fence with the slanted barbed wire across the top. Camp Roberts runs along next to the road for as far north as we can see, but we don't walk that way. We walk along the western side, where the fence climbs up into the hills that some people call golden but which are really just dead-weed brown.

Birds shriek far off in the scrawny oaks. Something feels wrong inside the backpack. Reminds me of when Manny's dog went on the freeway and we found the body and scraped it into a bag and the two of us carried it off into the hills and we buried the pieces of bone and fur.

"I suppose I should open the bag and check for damage," I say.

"Suppose." Manny swallows.

"Yeah . . ." Instead, we just keep walking. "Nothing we could do, anyway."

Near the back corner, there's a space where someone

ripped up the chain link. I crawl under. Manny pushes the bag through to me.

"You can wait out there," I say.

"I know," he says, crawling under. His shoulders and fat ass barely make it through, but I don't laugh at him. He stands, not bothering to brush off the dirt.

"Where do you think they are?" I ask.

Manny stares around, squints against the glare, and then shrugs.

We walk between long rows of boarded-up barracks. The gray-white wood looks like it could just curl up and burn. But even in this heat, it feels spooky like a ghost town. Maybe my dad wandered through these same barracks, when they were freshly painted, waiting to get shipped out. We keep walking.

"You know what 'Windowpane' means, don't you, Manny? Nino told you."

Manny stops.

"*Mierda*. You going to ask me about your dad now? Here?"

"There a better time? A better place?"

"Windowpane is acid, you know that. Made by this dude Owsley that Nino knew back when they were in the Haight hanging around the Dead. It can make you do stupid stuff."

"Like what stupid stuff?"

He stands with his arms crossed for a long, long time. I wait.

"Like fall off a bridge in Big Sur."

"Like he thought he could fly," I say.

"Something like that. It was that big one, the Bixby. You ready now?"

"Yeah. Let's do this."

We wander past a building that looks kind of like the barracks except it's smaller and the windows are long and arched and a steeple rises above double doors. A chapel.

"I think this is it," I say.

"He said barracks. This is a chapel."

"Hell, there's no better place for a chapel than here, when you think about it."

One of the double doors swings open about a foot.

"I don't like it." Manny is shaking. "A chapel ain't right."

But he follows me up the steps all the same.

"Ain't right? Hell, you tell me one thing. One thing. That's right about any of this."

I pull open the door. Bobby Martin stands just inside. I know right away that the Ace brought him as a lookout because Bobby and me used to be buddies. A message to me how deep he can get into my life. It gives me the creeps figuring he knows something about me that goes way back to fourth grade. There's no point in Bobby and me even pretending we don't know each other, so we both nod.

"Where is he?"

Bobby looks down the aisle into the dark.

There's a weird ocean swushing kind of sound all around me.

Sunlight peeks through slats in the boarded-up windows and sends streaks through the dusty air. There are rows of pews, most of them knocked over like dominoes. Everything else is gone. That ocean sound is coming from *inside* my head.

What if my father sat in this chapel, in that front pew that's still standing, praying before he went off to war?

I start walking down the aisle, feet slipping on the dusty floor. Manny waits at the door next to Bobby. Someone sits against the altar wall, and it don't take a genius to figure out who. The shadows of two Jokers stand on either side. The ocean sound in my head is quiet and peaceful, like lying in a sleeping bag listening to the waves over the dunes. A part of me is already curling up inside that bag just to get away from the for real, but I shake myself out of it, sucking air thick with dust like an acolyte has been swinging incense all around, only this is a dry, dead smell. The outline of a long-gone cross scars the wall above them.

I reach the front and stop. All three wear baseball caps so there's just shadows where the faces ought to be. The Ace sits on a crate like it's some kind of throne.

"Kneel," he says.

"What?"

"Kneel and lay the bag before me."

I do as he says. The ocean sound inside my head stops like when the water is building to one big mother wave, and it's so dead quiet I can hear Manny's throat clucking clear down at the other end of the chapel.

The Ace reaches out a long arm and undoes the drawstring, the bag falling away from the clock. "A clock. Antique maybe. A righteous choice, RJ. I knew you'd come through. A shame, really, you won't join us . . . What's this?" He lifts it and something metallic rattles against the wood. "Man, it's broken."

He drops it and sits back on the box. He takes off his hat and I swear I can almost hear his hand rubbing against those stubs and freckles and sweat.

The first wave comes pounding back in my head.

"It . . . it was a accident . . . We . . ."

"Shut up." He smiles. "You scared?"

He leans forward, chewing on his lower lip, chewing at my fear.

I nod.

"This stupid clock don't matter. We got bigger plans."

"What?"

"Be here one week from today with something else you stole from him."

"That ain't fair. You can't . . ."

"What did you say?"

I shut up.

"We'll make this our own little ritual. Any questions?"

"No."

"Didn't think so. Don't get up until we leave."

If only they'd beat me up, anything just so it would be over. Not fair. I stand, my knees shaking. Manny is beside me. He don't say anything. He lets me turn on my own and walk down the aisle toward the sunlight.

CHAPTER SEVENTEEN

UNFALLEN ANGELS

The water tank rises thirty feet over Mission Street, a huge white ball sitting on three green legs. ARCANGEL is written around the eastern side so that drivers clear over on the freeway can read it. Maybe they know it's the name of our town, or maybe they think it's some spiritual advertisement, or just maybe it's God's golf ball and He's about to tee off.

Manny and me are sitting on the shady west side of a catwalk edging the ball. My feet dangle as we look down at all the craziness of the preparations for the Fourth of July parade. I dig this free-fall feel of heights, the tingling in my legs, the creepy tilt like the water tank can just shrug me off . . .

"You're freaking me out," Manny says. He's so scared he presses his back against the tank like he'll melt right through it. Then again, closed-in spaces don't bother him at all.

"This ain't the Bixby, RJ."

I pretend I don't hear that. Looking down at all the people, it's like we're angels. Like nothing bad can touch us up here.

Nothing.

"Manny, you remember that teacher that went on and on about free will?"

"Father Speckler." Manny sucks air, his fists white-knuckling the rail.

"Yeah. Well, he said how free will was some kind of gift to us. That God was doing us a favor giving us free will even though it let evil into the world."

"RJ, you ain't getting me into another one of these talks. If you're gonna bag on God or the Church, you can just shut up."

"I didn't mean nothing by it. I was just looking at all the people down there and it's kind of like we're angels looking down on them. Then I was thinking about the Blackjacks and this weird thought hit me. Maybe God made free will just for His fun. If God cranks the world up and lets it go without knowing where it's headed, well that's got to be a whole lot more fun for Him."

"RJ, you're full of crap. You're hanging around that old man too much. It's making you weird."

Manny is right about that. I had hoped he'd do the sidekick thing with me to Leguin's, but he just don't fit in there. We're high enough to catch the breeze sliding over the mountains from the ocean, while down below the asphalt is baking in the sun.

The buildings on Mission are mostly just used-to-bes from when the highway came right through our town. Like the weekend produce stand that used to be a forties two-pump Spanish-style gas station. Or the New Light Gospel Covenant Cathedral, which used to be an old movie house and has just enough letters to spell out GOD IS LITE on the old marquee. Or

All-American Tires, SPECIALIZING IN RECONDITIONAL TREAD, which used to be a blacksmith with a really cool metal sculpture garden for hippies and tourists and now has tow trucks to troll the freeway.

Locals stand in clusters along the sidewalk. Two years ago, the parade was crazy huge for the bicentennial. But these last two years have been kind of a letdown. Abuelita sits on her beach chair like it's a throne, her granddaughters taking turns holding an umbrella over her. We both better pray she don't look up and see us. One person I don't see is Roxanne. The Fourth's one day her mom would always let her run free. But Roxanne is nowhere around. And no one even cares. People just say she ran away and that's the end of it.

Then I see them, with their Raiders caps, T-shirts, and greasy jeans. Blackjacks. People in the valley pretend the Blackjacks are just a figment. As long as people can pretend, the Blackjacks don't feel so scary.

Two red devil drum majors waving plastic pitchforks strut down the street. Our school banner reads, THE FIGHTING ANGELS. The little band follows, dressed in choir robes and halos.

Three Blackjacks cut in front of Davy Franklin on the sidewalk and push him around back of the Taco Den.

"Manny, did you see that? That deputy stared right at them and didn't do nothing."

"What do you expect, RJ? That's Meyers. Nino said he used to be a Blackjack himself."

"Yeah, I guess it makes sense," I say. "A Blackjack who's gotten too old don't have a lot of career options. Being a deputy would be pretty tempting to some guy who spent his kid years bullying people. And it gives the Blackjacks connections on the inside. But there must be some okay deputies."

"Sure. But can you trust which ones?" Manny shrugs. "And would a good sheriff even believe you, RJ? You're already a royal pain in his butt."

"Okay, don't rub it in."

The band is followed by a white Caddy convertible with Mayor Benny Brown sitting on the trunk above the back seat, waving.

"But what if we were to go to someone outside the valley?" Manny asks.

"What do you mean?"

"Well, like the sheriff or the police or whatever, over in San Luis or something," he says.

"Man, they don't have jurisdiction over what's going on here."

We let that hang between us.

The mayor is followed by kids pedaling bicycles decorated by red, white, and blue ribbon, baseball cards flicking the spokes, and American flags. We whistle down at Charley pedaling my Stingray like crazy. The 4-H straggles down the street, led by Fat Jack the jackass.

Standing in a flatbed truck that's draped in bunting are the Bobby Soxers, our town's only sports claim to fame, having finished runner-up at State. Theresa is the star. Manny and me go to all her games. I always hope for the other team to get a runner on first. Then our pitcher, Bertha, will whip a sinker and the batter will smack a grounder up the middle, but Theresa's long legs will run it down and she'll toe second and then lift and spin and toss across her chest and double the runner at first. It is the only time I can stand and shout, "Theresa, you're beautiful!" and Manny, instead of slugging my shoulder, he has to high-five me. Now, like she has some kind of radar, she looks straight up at me and waves.

Uniformed VFWs end the parade. Nino-'n-Smitty, wearing jeans and their Marine jackets, walk with them. They could've been near the front of the parade riding their hogs with flags and banners flying. But here they are at the end walking with these old guys from the VFW.

"If my dad were alive," I say, "he'd be walking there, too."

"Right on," Manny says.

The town falls in behind the vets as the parade wanders to the picnic grounds.

Manny is squirming to get down now, but I could stay up here always.

"Manny, I hear Roxanne is missing. You think the Blackjacks done something to her?" Manny won't look at me. "Manny?"

"'Buelita says I shouldn't talk about her with you."

"With me?" I ask. "Why the hell not?"

"You don't know?"

"If I knew, I wouldn't ask."

"Well, she just said don't." Manny clutches the rail and gets up like he's going to head down the ladder with or without me. I stay seated, waving my legs in space.

Manny sighs and sits back down. "With the parade over, someone is gonna see us up here."

"Maybe Roxanne joined some cult," I say. "Like your *tía* with that Peoples Temple."

"Don't talk about my *tía*," he says.

"I ain't. I'm talking about Roxanne."

"Okay, then. Roxanne could do just about any crazy thing, RJ."

"But a cult?"

"You're the one who thought Jim Jones was so cool when he was here on that housing thing," he says. "With those sunglasses and that suit. And people say he's a cult leader."

"I said he *looked* cool."

"Same dif."

"Not hardly."

"Well, you can't blame my *tía*. Even your Sanders worked with Jones."

"He's not *my* Sanders," I say. "And he had to work with him. Jones was the head of the freaking housing authority, and Mr. Sanders was working with migrants."

"Why you arguing, RJ?" Manny gets up. "The Peoples Temple cult ain't even in San Francisco no more." He creeps along the catwalk to the ladder. "They're in South America on some commune." He climbs over and then looks back at me. "And Roxanne ain't leaving this valley."

"You feel like going up to the old mission aqueduct? We haven't been up there in a long time. We could watch the fireworks from off eagle rock. Like old times."

"Yeah, RJ." His voice has softened. "I'd like that. Like old times."

I get up and follow him back down into the for real world.

CHAPTER EIGHTEEN
KABOOM

It's almost sundown when Manny and me are walking up the canyon along Indian Trail Road with the foothills on our left and the valley spread out to our right. It's the best place to catch the fireworks. Clouds off the ocean make a ripply sky ceiling, and there's this weird light the color of my bronzed baby shoes.

"You haven't carried Charley with us since that night with the blood," Manny says.

"We don't need him tagging along."

"That don't sound like you, RJ."

"Well, it's better he's not with us if the Blackjacks show up," I say.

"Have you seen how he's growing?" Manny asks. "In a few years, he'll be taller than you. Won't that be weird?"

"Well, then he can carry my ass for a change."

Indian Trail Road used to be dirt winding along the foothills. Now the road is gooey new asphalt warming the soles of my Chucks. There are rocks below the trail that are all that's left of the old Mission aqueduct. Manny and me used to hike to the end of this trail where there's the remains of a dam they say was built by the Chumash. In late spring, there used to be enough water in the pond above the rocks to swim in.

"Those were great times up at the dam, huh, Manny?"

"The greatest."

"Let's go up there after."

"After what?"

I shrug.

"It'll be dried out," he says.

Then we're stopped by a gate blocking our way. A wrought-iron sign arches between Spanish stucco pillars flanking the road: INDIAN TRAIL ESTATES. Iron gates wrapped with a chain lock us out. A wall runs in either direction.

"You know about this, Manny?"

He shrugs. "It's the first housing tract in the valley."

"Yeah, no kidding."

"Nino-'n-Smitty tried to get work here," Manny says. "But they wouldn't hire."

"They'd work here, on this?"

"It's a living."

"Hell it is." I shake the heavy chain.

"Look over there." Manny points to the right.

Three cars are parked on a visitors pad outside the wall. Fancy cars. A souped-up Bug, a baby blue Toyota pickup, and an old teardrop Porsche.

"Those ain't locals," I say.

"Maybe we better leave," Manny says. "See that NO TRESPASSING sign?"

"No way." There's plenty of slack in the chain, so I slip through.

"That's trespassing," Manny warns.

"You think they can make us trespassers on our own childhood? Get your ass in here."

He shrugs and slips in.

Streets have been laid out in sharp angles and small circles. There's even a sign that points down Pocahontas Lane. Concrete slabs have been poured for each house. Two-by-four framing rises like dinosaur bones on most of the slabs. We walk to the end of a cul-de-sac near the valley ridge, where there's a slab that's bigger than the rest. This could be the best chance I ever get to stand inside a mansion, even if it's just getting built, so I step through the framing that's going to be the front door.

"RJ, what are you doing? Let's just get out of here."

"I gotta check this out."

Manny hops onto the slab after me. Manny's MO is to make the best of a bad situation. That's why he's searching the ground around the electrical boxes for slugs we can buff and then slip into the slot in the old Coke machine outside the New Light. The sun is finally setting into a muggy warm that feels like breathing into a Folgers can.

"We shoulda brought flashlights," Manny says.

I wander through the framing of the unbuilt mansion. Our trailer would fit into what's probably going to be the living room. There's a second story and a higher part that could be some kind of loft.

"RJ, those are Slows over there." He points to some college kids at the edge of the ridge. "Slows" means guys who go to the college over in San Luis Obispo. They don't usually come slumming into the valley. But when they do, it's never good.

"Manny, I bet we could fit the Silverstream into this one room. And I bet there'll be less people living in this whole house than live in my trailer."

"Figuring there are seven people in your trailer, that's a pretty good guess," he says.

"Don't that piss you off?" I ask.

He shrugs. "I don't live in a trailer. Let's get out of here."

"We'll miss the fireworks."

"We can watch them on the way back."

A fancy-colored window has already been framed into the second story. I grab a chunk of concrete and heft it, feeling an itch to throw it at the glass. Then the last sunlight touches it and it shimmers like stained glass in a church, so I don't bother.

"Hey, you punks. What are you doing here?" a big kid calls.

"Now you done it," Manny says.

We could run, of course. But no Slows are going to chase me out. We strut over to where they've turned the front of a slab overlooking the valley into party central, with beach chairs, coolers, blankets, and a sliced watermelon. Their radio is blasting the Bee Gees.

Three girls are waving sparklers, the sparks dancing off the slab and drifting on the evening breeze.

"You shouldn't do that. You could cause a brush fire," I say.

Two of the girls are tall, with frosted and feathered hair, hip-hugger bell-bottoms, and halter tops. They might be Charlie's Angels wannabes, but they don't look like no angels in this valley. The third is more of a Velma from *Scooby-Doo*. Short redhead with freckles and big boobs. Instead of a sweater covering them like in the cartoon, she wears a ruffly blouse with a gold crucifix nestled in the valley between the lacy edges of her bra. Now, that is a shrine if ever I saw one. I don't care what Mr. Sanders would have said, I'd take a pilgrimage to that crucifix any day.

"What you staring at, punk?" The guy has a flattop that makes him look like Frankenstein's monster. He's not very tall, but he's got shoulders and arms as big as Nino's. And mean, squinty eyes. If he had grown up here, he'd be a Blackjack. But he didn't grow up here, so he's just some bully. The other two guys are a matching set to the Charlie's Angels. They wear bell-bottoms and heeled cowboy boots. They got blond mullets and neat horseshoe mustaches. The flattop bully comes at us with a fake smile and two slices of watermelon.

"Eddy, no," the redhead says.

The others laugh.

"Try some of this," he says.

I shrug and grab the big slice from this Eddy guy, and Manny grabs the other. A *kaboom* shakes the valley. Perfect timing.

"Listen, Eddy," the redhead says. "The fireworks are about to start. Leave the boy alone."

Boy? She could at least have said "kid" or "dude" or "punk" or something. Boy? I stuff the watermelon in my mouth and the sweet juice trickles down my throat and then begins to burn.

"Go . . . go . . . go . . ." The guys laugh.

My mouth catches fire. Manny is choking. This watermelon

is spiked. Tequila, maybe. But even Nino never let me have any, so I'm not sure.

A firework explodes and colors drip across the sky. I spit out seeds and shrug like the sting is no big deal. I take another bite. Another *kaboom*, but my eyes are shut, so I miss the colors. The taste is not so bad if you're expecting it. Kind of sweet and not as hot as 'Buelita's sausages. I hold my breath and shove that last big chunk into my mouth, sticky juices dribbling down my chin.

The girls grab the guys' arms and pull them back to the fireworks show.

"I'm tired of this," Manny says. "Let's go."

"Just one more piece of this watermelon," I say.

"Bad idea, RJ." He sighs. "But what else is new?"

That's how come we're still standing there when the finale slaughters the sky in color, and there's no way I want to leave until that's finished, and Manny was right, because those three Slows now have us surrounded.

"So what should we do with these trespassers?" Eddy asks.

"Leave my friend RJ alone." The Ace steps out of the shadows. He's backed by Jokers, including the ones that followed me at the Stardust. Buns stands behind them. He don't look like a Joker yet, but he's pretty much lost.

The redhead—I can't take my eyes off that crucifix—is looking at me in a new light, thinking I'm with the Blackjacks. God, I'm ashamed that she thinks I'm a part of *them*. Then I'm even more ashamed because I *am* a part of them. Not in the way she thinks it. But in the way any victim is a part of his tormentor. Shame is a weird, sick feeling.

"Who the hell are these guys?" one of the blond guys asks through his mustache, pointing at Brent Keating.

"The Blackjacks," I say.

The Slows are the same size as the Blackjacks, and probably more athletic. But if it comes to a fight, the Slows don't stand no more chance than a golden retriever against hungry coyotes. No chance at all against something that dark and wild.

"You know you're trespassing." Eddy faces off against the Ace. He don't get how much danger they're in.

"And you're not . . . trespassing?" the Ace asks.

"We got permission to be here. My uncle is the developer."

"Ah, the developer," the Ace says in a mocking voice.

"Eddy," the redhead says. "Let's go."

"You guys don't get it, do you?" the Ace says. "About who's the trespassers."

One of the Slows pulls Eddy's arm. "He isn't worth it."

"Did you enjoy the watermelon, RJ?" The Ace is still looking at Eddy, not me. The Ace don't care about that watermelon at all. He's asking me just to show he's been here since the beginning, just been biding his time.

"It was okay." I shrug. "No big."

"The watermelon and the trespassing remind me of a story," the Ace says. "There was this old farmer who had a little watermelon patch. He loved those watermelons and didn't share them with anyone. The boys in the valley loved that watermelon, too. It tasted all the sweeter being stole fruit, as they say. So that old man stuck a sign in the watermelon patch. What do you suppose it said?"

"NO TRESPASSING?" the redhead says quickly. I can tell she thinks their best chance to get out of this is to humor the Ace.

"Ya think?" the Ace mocks. "How is that old man gonna enforce no trespassing? Tell a cop? Would a cop bother about a couple kids stealing a watermelon? Those cops probably did it themselves as kids. They might even be thinking, *Give it up, Gramps. Let them have one. You can't eat them all.* Or maybe the old man would shoot the kids himself? He could be that crazy. But this ain't about crazy. No, the sign read: ONE OF THESE WATERMELONS HAS BEEN SPIKED WITH POISON."

"Very clever," Eddy says. "We're done here."

"Oh, that's not the punch line. The next day the old man goes out to his watermelon patch. It looks like not a single watermelon has been stolen. Then he notices the sign. It's been changed. The 'one' has been crossed out and 'two' has been scrawled in its place. God, I love the simplicity of it. You have five minutes." The Ace never changes the tone in his voice. "Five minutes to get your shit out of here or you will regret ever hearing about this valley."

As they gather their stuff, the redhead slips her crucifix back under her blouse. Then they're dragging beach chairs and coolers through the slabs and frames, the girls wobbling on their platform shoes. Manny and me turn to slip away.

"Where you going, RJ?"

"Home," I say.

"You haven't forgot, have you?" The Ace still has that dead, flat tale-teller voice. "Your next delivery? After all, we just gave you some protection."

"Nah. I haven't forgot."

"I have faith in you, RJ."

Then they're gone.

"Manny, what do ya think was the moral to the Ace's story?"

"There ain't nothing moral in him," Manny says. "So why

do you think the Blackjacks were out here?" Manny asks. "Were they following you?"

We're making our way down Indian Trail in the dark.

"Nah. I ain't that important. Life just has its twists."

And one of those twists means another visit to Leguin. And another visit to him means having to finish a tale I should never have started.

CHAPTER NINETEEN

MELTING BLUES

I'm sitting at the top of the hill on the Stingray, scoping the old man's place from the same spot where Roxanne and I sat, it feels like a million years ago. Dark afternoon clouds lie across Big Mama, but it's only a rain tease. There hasn't been a drop since the downpour the day the old man arrived. My head still throbs from that spiked watermelon last night.

Mrs. Elliot had said that Roxanne brought that clock from Mr. Leguin's. Had Roxanne stolen it or had he given it to her? And how much does he know about her disappearance?

I slalom down the hill, letting the tires slide and dig into the weeds and dirt with each turn as I take my own sweet time. I cruise round by way of the root cellar. The door is padlocked. I lean against the angled door, my cheek resting against the splintered wood, and listen.

Silence.

"Roxanne?"

More silence. A creepy feeling oozes up out of the air vent

and slides down into my belly, trailing a sweet, musty smell. This is stupid. She's not there. No one is down there.

I walk the bike past the barn and see Leguin sitting in his chair staring out through the screen door. I let the old bike drop and I hop up the steps. A bottle and two glasses sit on the table next to him like he knows I'm coming. How long has he been hunched over that cane, eyeballing that screen, waiting for me to show?

I open the screen and step in.

"Sit," he says.

I plop down in the soft chair he won't sit in because he can't get out of it. He just gives me that stare, and I get that sudden creepy feeling, like he's got me picked for something.

"No more sherry," I say. After last night, I figure I'll never try booze again.

Leguin nods and recorks the bottle, not even pouring some for himself.

"Did you enjoy a pleasant Fourth of July?"

"Sure," I say, "how about you?"

"I celebrate the Fourteenth of July."

It figures that he'd have to do things different. "Why the Fourteenth?"

"Bastille Day."

"Bastille Day?"

"You might say it's the French Fourth of July."

I stare at all the antiques cramming the room. Why can't I steal from him? What's wrong with me? We can go until tomorrow just sitting here without talking. There's a blank space on the mantel over the fireplace. It's the spot where you usually see a clock in old movies.

"There's this lady in town, her name is Mrs. Elliot." I'm not sure how far I'm going with this, but now that I've jumped, there's only the bottom. "She owns Mrs. Elliot's Antiques and Collectibles Emporium."

Leguin is quiet.

"She sells old stuff. You know, like antique clocks."

"Indeed."

"She had this clock for sale that she said was yours."

"Did she?"

"She said that this girl named Roxanne stole it from you."

"Roxanne, you say?"

"Yeah . . ."

"And you saw this clock?"

"Yeah. It was an antique that would fit perfect in that empty space over your fireplace there."

I wait. No answer.

"She's been missing more than a week and a day," I continue. "Some people think she ran away. But I don't believe it. And I think you know something about her."

His melting blue eyes freeze up into cubes.

There's a whole long silence.

"I believe you have a tale to finish, young man."

So here we go.

"A tale?"

"Yes, something to do with that priest . . ."

"Father Speckler."

"Yes. And a science demonstration, and your Mr. Sanders—"

"He ain't *my* Mr. Sanders."

He steeples his hands and stares through me.

How is it possible to need to tell something, yet not want to tell it, all at the same time?

"Okay, but we ain't done with Roxanne. If I tell some, you got to tell some back."

"*Très bon.*"

I feel kind of light-headed as the tale rises up out of me and I can't stop it no more than a dry heave.

The Tale of the Love Souvenirs and My Old Soul

When I went to school that following Monday after Mr. Sanders had put the idea in my head for my demonstration, I didn't mess up or say one "Father" before lunch 'cause I couldn't handle that dark little closet no more. But the more Father Speckler figured I wouldn't talk back, the harder he rode me. I went home for lunch and came back late, carrying baby Peanut, with the twins trying to keep up behind me. Amy and Charley, who also went to Our Lady's, were waiting in that empty hall like I told them. I could hear Father Speckler inside going on with his God's children *number, and I waited for my cue, and it came when he said, "Just where is Mr. Armante? Truant in order to avoid his demonstration?"*

That's when we paraded in. I lined the sibs up in front of the class and had each of them hold up a picture of their father. Amy was the only one I had a hard time getting to do it. But if you'd seen her father, you'd understand.

Father Speckler demanded, "You have an explanation for all this?"

"Yes, Father," I said. "They are my Science Project Demonstration. As you can see, each of them sort of looks like their prospect. Well, my dad left me this here Hohner harmonica and eight hundred dollars when he died. I tried to sell it once, but my mom wouldn't let me." I sucked in a few notes, sort of a blues tune. "I figure that eight hundred bucks lasted me till I was five years, seven months. So I owe my mom for three years, eight months. That's 'cause my dad is the only prospect who don't pay some child support. You see, Father, it all started with my mom's streak of bad luck. Her

131

first prospect, my father, died. Her second didn't marry her officially on account of he was already married and forgot to tell her. The third beat her up. So she was three kids in before she knew what was going down. I guess that turned her off to getting married. Like she says, she don't trust her own judgment."

Father Speckler wrote a note and grabbed a kid to take it to the office.

"I like to call us kids 'love souvenirs,'" I said. "It's like my mom loves the prospect, and she wants something lasting to remember him by. Of course, marriage don't last. But kids, they last—if you take good care of them. I guess she figures that if she don't trust her own judgment and marry them, she could at least have a souvenir." I blew some more notes.

Manny was sitting in the front row. He had his face buried in his hands and was peeking through the fingers like at a gross accident you don't want to see but can't help looking.

"But souvenirs ain't cheap," I said. "So I figure it's only right that the prospects pay. And most of them don't even mind, my mom being such a wonderful person and they love her even after they find out she don't trust her own judgment."

Father Speckler had stopped hopping. Standing still he looked even smaller. Just then, Mother Catherine walked in and stood in the back of the room with her arms folded across her chest.

"So you can see, there are six of us souvenirs," I continued, "counting me and counting the twins as two. I'm the oldest, then there's Amy, who's three years younger than me, and right behind her came Charley, though you wouldn't know it 'cause they're so different. Then the twins. Finally, there's Peanut, who's only just one." Peanut let out a gurgle in Amy's

arms right on cue. "My mom had thought her prospecting days were over, if you know what I mean."

Mother Catherine started down the aisle and the whole class sucked air and I clutched Peanut for protection. She led us in a regular pilgrimage down to the office. First she called my mom at work to come down and pick us all up. Then she pulled me in the office while the others waited outside.

I just toed that line and grabbed the foot of Jesus and held on. But nothing happened. I looked back under my armpit and Mother Catherine was sitting behind her desk staring at my backside. I couldn't understand it. I mean, I was a regular in that office for a whole lot worse. What was the big deal? She just sat there.

"Sister Phyllis had such hopes for you," Mother Catherine said. "Didn't you, Sister?"

"One of the brightest children we have ever had," Sister Phyllis said. "An old soul, I like to think."

Then Mother Catherine sighed and said, "You don't seem to fit in here at Our Lady's. I just pray that you do find a place to fit in. So very much promise. I'll call down to Sixth Street Elementary and let them know you will be arriving on Monday."

Sixth Street was actually uphill. But to Mother Catherine it was always down.

That evening I went to Mr. Sanders's trailer to tell him how the demonstration turned out. I figured he should get part of the blame for putting the idea in my head. But he wasn't sitting outside on his slab like usual. I knocked, but there was no answer, and so I opened the door. That's how come I found his body. He'd stopped eating food, I guess, and so the booze had eaten his liver instead.

I was in that trailer in the dark with . . . with that thing. I couldn't move. Couldn't even find my way out of that little space. Then I saw one of those round Canterbury pictures hung on the wall. It was that fat Bath lady on a horse. I couldn't remember her tale. Then I edged to the next pilgrim, a scrawny priest on a donkey. The Pardoner, maybe. And so I followed them all the way to the door and I was free.

CHAPTER TWENTY
TUMBLER

"RJ," Leguin interrupts, "I am truly . . ."

"Don't you dare say it."

He nods and shuts up.

"So I stole the YOURE HOOSTE sign. No one else would've wanted it, anyway. Yeah, I was shook. And don't give me none of that father-figure garbage. If I'd wanted a father figure I wouldn't have picked no drunk that hardly no one could get close to on account of the smell. I still make sure that CANTE BURY stays lit."

Who the hell is Leguin to feel sorry for *me*?

"Why do you even care?" I ask. "What do my stories mean to you?"

Silence.

"I have something to show you," he finally says. "Help me up."

I'm almost used to that loose skin as I pull him up by the wrist. The old man hobbles down the steps, not even looking back he's so sure I'm following. There's a pink tinge along the horizon. He's walking straight for that root cellar and my mouth goes dry and drops into my belly and there's a freaking earthquake in my head and my legs feel weak. But I'm right behind him.

Leguin shuffles past the root cellar and heads around to the front of the barn. The sun is doing its long slide into sunset. The summer heat is oozing out of the warped gray boards. The old man stops at this door hanging by one hinge. An animal sound whispers from the dark behind that door and I'm wondering if the old man's secret hasn't been in here all along. A smell of dry rot. No, this might be a piece of the secret, but the big chunk is still holed up in that root cellar.

He shoves the door open with his shoulder and this dank-animal-nest sort of smell lies in there. It's cool, almost inviting. We step inside, facing a rustling, clicking sound. There's a cooing that makes me think of lying on the porch in the dark and listening to my mom with one of her prospects in the trailer, but I won't think about that. Light pokes through cracks between the boards, dusting the room in pink streaks. Of course, the sound is just some kind of bird. There's a big square shadow in the far corner.

"Man, it's a stupid old birdcage."

"A coop," he says, stepping over to it.

"What?"

"A coop. Not a cage. A coop."

"I knew that."

"Open the door."

I can't find the door in all that chicken wire. Finally, I feel the latch and flick it open. A head pokes from a hole in a box at the back of the coop.

"Shit," I say. "It's only a pigeon."

"Watch your language."

"Sorry."

The old man's claw reaches inside and taps on the wood floor. One of the birds—there're two—hops over and rubs against his hand. He wraps his claws around it and lifts it out as gentle as holding a baby.

"Get the Old Tumbler," he says.

"What?"

"Lord, child, you can be slow. Pick up the other bird."

I reach in and grab it, but the sucker twists all around and I let go 'cause the wings feel so thin they could just snap.

"Wrap one hand around each side of his body, right over the wings. Do it firmly so that his wings are pinned down. His neck should stick out between your thumbs."

I try. But the bird is freaked now and it has some pretty slick moves.

"Don't be afraid. Just grab him."

Well, I'm not afraid of a stupid pigeon. So I just reach out, catch it by a leg, and wrap my hands around the wings. "I did it!"

"Fine. Let's take them outside."

The sunset has faded into a deep blue. I feel that bird trembling in my hands like I'm holding on to a feathered heart.

"*L'heure bleue,*" Leguin whispers. He's holding his bird with one of his clawed hands as we walk around the side, and he's scratching that soft spot under its neck and the bird makes cooing sounds and rubs against him.

"What did you say?"

"*L'heure bleue.* The blue hour. That is what we called this time when I was a child."

The thought of him as a kid is just too weird.

Leguin reaches in his suit pocket, pulls out a seed, puts it between his teeth, and that bird takes it right out of his mouth. Watching it feels kind of like looking down at a couple making out in their car at the Stardust. He's nuts if he thinks I'll do weird things with mine. But he just leads me around to the front yard. We reach the gravel drive, and the old man gives that whistle laugh and looks over at me like he's surprised I'm still there.

He lobs that bird like he's tossing a ball to a four-year-old. He looks over at me, so I throw my bird and step back, not wanting it to fly right over my head and shit on me. Both birds shoot straight up until they're just specks at the tip-top of that dark blue. I squint so as not to lose sight. It looks like they come to a stop. Like that second when you reach the top on a roller coaster, and it just sort of nudges over the edge and you look down and down and down and there's nothing between you and dying. Then the specks start sliding down that sky and I can't take my eyes off them.

One of the birds flips over and starts tumbling out of control. I look around, thinking that maybe a Blackjack shot it. But the old man, he has that smile on his face, and I know it's nothing like that. The other bird is flip-flopping down to the ground. I always figured people were the only kind of animal that killed themselves, except for maybe those lemmings. Flip-flop, flip-flop. There's no way they'll make it. Man, that old guy is one cold dude. Here, his birds that he's raised since they were eggs are heading straight down to be sunny-side up, and he's grinning.

I'm hooked. I don't know whether to watch the birds crashing or that sick grin. They're level with the trees now, going about a million miles per, and they're having this change of heart, flipping over, trying to pull out. Of course, it's too late. They're about to eat it.

Then they pull back hard on their tail feathers into this beautiful slo-mo tilt and just a couple feet from the ground swoop back up and head for the sky to do it all over.

The old man looks over at me. "I had a feeling that you would appreciate it." He says it almost like I'd just passed some kind of test or something.

"Why do they do it?" I ask when I get my voice back.

"There are a few theories based upon genetics and survival and the like, but I believe they do it simply for the pure enjoyment of the act."

"Yeah," I say. "Amazing."

"Amazing Grace. That's the name of the female."

I look over to see if that was an on-purpose joke. But the old man is just staring up at the birds. We stand there watching until it gets too dark and he makes this clicking sound and they fly back to him.

We carry them to the barn.

"I want you to take them." Mr. Leguin don't look at me.

"I don't want . . ."

Then I glance close at him and see there's no point in arguing. He probably figures he's getting too old to take care of them. And who knows, maybe if Amazing Grace has some eggs, then I could sell the babies. God, I need the cash.

Leguin shuffles through the dark barn and puts them in a portable cage he's got next to the coop.

"During your days in grammar school, RJ, were you taught about the veneration of relics?"

"What does that . . . yeah, Father Speckler taught us something about them."

"The Jesuit in your tale?"

"Yeah, him."

"What did he say?"

"Well, relics could be things like a piece of the cross or the grail, or they could be saints' bones, that kind of thing. People, mostly in the old days, gave money to a priest to worship the relic, and then they'd get absolution, or maybe even a miracle would happen to them. That sounded pretty awesome."

"Indeed."

"But the truth is that relics are probably just a slick rip-off. What do I know? I got kicked out in fourth grade, so maybe if I'd stayed around longer I could have learned more about it."

Leguin hands me a fluffy gray pigeon feather.

"My favorite reliquary tale," he says, "is the story of a medieval relic that was reputed to be the feather from the wing of an archangel. Imagine that."

I wait for him to tell that story, but he just turns and heads out. That's cold, leaving me hanging.

So I pick up the portable cage, stumble out into the night, and strap it between the Stingray's handlebars. I walk the bike down to the main road and he follows me. He must really love these old birds.

"You don't have a light on your bike," he says.

"I got twenty-twenty night vision."

"I'll file you as a class-one insurance hazard." That whistle laugh.

The bike wobbles a little with the extra weight as I start to pedal. Chain, don't fail me now.

"Richard."

I swoop back around to the gate, figuring he's got some last-minute advice on their feeding or something. I can't remember when someone used my for real name.

"Roxanne was here three times." The way he wheezes, I'm not sure I hear him right. "I gave her the clock."

CHAPTER TWENTY-ONE
GRUNION

Manny and me are walking along the frontage road, taking our sweet time in the heat on our way home after another delivery to the Blackjacks at Camp Roberts. We're walking 'cause Nino-'n-Smitty are on a job outside the valley. This time I'd bought a sculpture of a pretty lady's head to pretend I stole. Mrs. Elliot had called it a bust. I don't know how it could've been a bust, because I had been told that "bust" was a word you were supposed to use instead of "tits," but this sculpture didn't go below her neck, so there weren't no tits. I'd told Mrs. Elliot that if the tits weren't showing, then it really was a bust. That's a paradox. She didn't get it.

"How long you think you can keep these deliveries up, RJ? It's gotta end somewhere."

"Yeah, don't it?"

"At least you ought to get a new backpack." Manny points at the crusty pig's blood on the flaps.

Nino-'n-Smitty's truck rumbles at us so fast there's no

point trying to dodge it. Smitty sticks his face out the window and shows crooked teeth at us.

"Thought you was in Monterey," Manny says. "At that fish-packing place."

"We got canned." Smitty laughs at his own joke. With his crooked teeth, stringy beard, and giant Adam's apple, Smitty's got the ugliest laugh you'll ever hear. You can't help liking him.

"Grunion are running, *hombres*," Nino's gravelly voice booms from the shadow of the cab. "Hop in back."

Manny climbs up the stake gates, but I don't.

"We cleared it with your mom, RJ," Nino says. "Hell, she said you needed the R and R. She's worried about you, *mijo*."

I crawl over the stake gate, and the shift of the gears throws me onto the truck bed. Smitty rides with his head out the shotgun side, that stringy beard blowing, the Dead blasting, and his tattooed arm pounding the beat against the outside door.

Smitty bangs on the back window and points to crabs sliding around the bed and at the trash can roped against the stake gates. The smell of saltwater sloshing and the sound of claws scraping plastic. As the truck rumbles onto the freeway, we're sliding one way trying to grab the loose crabs by the feet and fling them with one move into that can without getting pinched. And the crabs are sliding away from us, wanting even more than us to get free. And all the time we're dodging sleeping bags, duffels, and a cooler.

As we snag the last of the crabs, the truck eases off the freeway and up the grade to the top of Big Mama. We stand up behind the cab sucking in that cool air that hits just when the truck noses over the top of the grade and starts that long slide down to Highway One and the ocean.

Manny and me got a new favorite song, so we scream out to the sky: *I want to fly like an eagle, to the sea. Fly like an eagle, let my spirit carry me!*

We head north on Highway One, between San Simeon and Big Sur. You could get busted for camping out on the beach, but Nino-'n-Smitty know this spot where you can pull off on the land side, then drive the truck through this gully and then cross under the highway at this arched bridge, and pull the truck up behind these rocks along the beach.

Nino-'n-Smitty make us set up camp. They grab a couple beers and strip down to their jeans. I don't remember ever seeing them without greasy old jeans. They sit by the water and let the waves slosh around their feet.

We're in a long cove with the waves foaming over rocks at either end. Even on this sunny day, the water swirls all icy greens. That water is never warm. Manny and me strip to our boxers and jump in. We know that after a couple beers Nino-'n-Smitty will throw us in anyway, and this way we got some dry clothes when we get out.

After we can't stand the cold water no more, we run along the hard sand at the edge, our feet going numb splashing in the foam. That funky kelp smell. The waves pounding. A breeze rips out of the ocean feeling like it's sucking my skin inside out.

It's still daylight, but Smitty has a fire going by the time we get back. There's a rusty grill over some rocks and a pot of water set to boil. We put our butts up close to the fire. Nino tosses us our jeans, and I catch mine just before a leg hits the fire.

When the water gets to boiling, Smitty throws in some crabs and we sit back as the sun begins to set. There's a rumble in the sand, and then from up the wash rolls this hippie bus that's straight out of Nino-'n-Smitty's good-old-biker-days stories. The front, all the way from the grill to the windows, is caked with dirt and grease. The body is so faded and dirty that I'm only a couple feet away before I make out the swirls of peace signs and animals and waves and all that kind of stuff.

I'm standing there staring when I finally figure out this one picture is a for real face staring down at me from one of the greasy windows. The head is shaved, but I can't tell if it's a him or a her. It looks young, but there's something old, like around the edges, that makes me not sure. It just keeps staring down at me without any expression as that window glows redder and redder in the sunset. Finally, the sky is dark and the face is gone. The bus door sighs open and out steps a whole family of hippies that look like they've driven right out of some time warp. But the weirdest thing is their shaved heads. Nino gives them the invite to our fire and food.

We all sit around the fire and don't say much. The mom and dad look older than Nino-'n-Smitty, but Nino knows the man from way back because the guy lived in Arcangel as a kid. The face that was in the window turns out to be a girl about my age. There's a little boy, and a two-year-old with a T-shirt and nothing else, which I guess saves them on diapers.

They're all skinny except for these little bellies. Their eyes are sunk-in black hollows in their faces. It's like the creepiest clan this side of the Addams Family. The kids tear the crabs apart to get the meat, but the mother, she won't touch them. I smile at the girl, who's pretty in a freakish kind of way. But she just chews on the crab and stares at the fire. Nino holds out a beer and the man takes it and Smitty shares a joint with him.

I lie back in the sand outside the circle of bodies hunched around the fire, and I let the muffled pounding of the waves drown out these stories I heard before, like about the Merry Pranksters and that guy Kesey and the acid tests, and so my mind is wandering away from that stuff by staring at the girl's pretty face in the firelight, picturing her framed by long blond hair, and a word jumps out of the talk and punches my gut—"Blackjacks."

"So, the Blackjacks are still around?" the man asks.

"You expected different?" Smitty asks right back.

"Nah. I was almost a Blackjack." The man tokes his joint. Silence.

"I ain't proud of it. Then my dad got work in Salinas, thinking that was safer. But there's parts of Salinas now that might be worse. The Soledad prison gang wars. Them dudes are so badass they could maybe clean out the Blackjacks if it came down to a turf war. But it feels like there's something else up in that gorge, you know? Something that can take hold and twist anything." He tries to laugh, but it's fake. "Hell, Danny, I thought you'd end up a Blackjack." It's funny hearing someone call Nino by his for real name. "But I can see now, you didn't. If someone wants to put an end to those creeps, I say more power to them. But a new gang will just take their place. Human nature, is all."

"There ain't much human left in them," Smitty says.

I wait for Nino to stand up and shout them down, but he just shrugs. How can he sit there and agree with that? I stare at his huge shoulders and at the tattoos that in this twilight are just pools, and I want to jump on his back and hit him, but then I want Nino to laugh and shrug me off like he did when I was little, and I want it to be like it was when Manny and me wrestled with him in the grass as little boys.

The wind kicks up and we all huddle close around the fire. It's creepy, all of us just staring around each other and not talking. Finally, the lady nods at us, stands up, and walks back to the bus. The man fumbles around in his pocket, digs out a couple of old joints, and hands them to Nino. Nino nods thanks, and the man and the kids shuffle back to the bus. Nino stares at the joints. Sniffs them. Rolls them around in his fingers. And then he does something I never thought I'd see. He throws them into the fire.

"Done with this shit," he says. "Let's get us some grunion."

Nino-'n-Smitty head down to the water in about the worst mood I ever seen them in. We follow, running up and down the beach, playing our flashlights along the glowing fingers of waves, but finding no grunion. I don't think Nino-'n-Smitty are even looking.

Finally, we figure out that Nino-'n-Smitty are gone and we head back to the fire. Their voices are whispering through the wind and we can hear them talking about the good old days as we reach the dune and slide down to the fire. But the way they're talking, it for sure don't sound like no good old days. Manny and me sit without interrupting.

"You know we don't drop acid or none of that no more?" Smitty asks us.

Manny shrugs.

"We catch you with even one joint," Nino says, "and we'll kick your ass."

"I hear you," Manny says.

I just nod, the words drying up in my throat as I think about Windowpane. I stare at kelp smoldering in the flames and the smoke stings my eyes and I knuckle away the tears. It takes me a while to build up to what I say next.

"That bridge. The Bixby," I say. "It's near here."

"You told him?" Nino asks Manny.

Manny shrugs.

"Yeah," Nino says. "It's a couple miles north up One."

"We can take you in the morning, if you want," Smitty says. "You're old enough."

The fire snaps.

"Nah. I'm good."

"You tell us. Anytime. We go." Nino says.

"Thanks. It happened a long time ago. I'm over it."

Waves pound on the other side of the dunes.

"Hey!" Manny says. "Listen. I think I hear a grunion."

Nino-'n-Smitty go quiet, listening.

Manny cuts a huge fart.

They break up laughing and switch from beer to Wild Turkey and they're not in a bad mood no more. We kick back in our sleeping bags against the dune, hunkering down against the wind. The fire smells like salt and kelp.

"Manny," I whisper. "What if Abuelita found out all that Nino-'n-Smitty were doing out here with you and me along?"

Manny shrugs. "She knows everything, so she'll find out about this, too. They'll have to pay for it somehow, but they'll think it's worth it. She also knows we're near the Bixby. This might have even been her idea."

"She hasn't told us a tale in a long time, since way before this summer," I say.

"She's sort of done with us, RJ." He squirms like there's sand in some weird places. "Not in a bad way. Like we've outgrown that stuff."

"You never outgrow stories," I whisper.

"It's not—"

"Did you ever hear about Cesar Aguilar?" Nino interrupts our whispering in his lowest, scariest voice.

Of course we have.

"No," we say.

"Cesar Aguilar was the last kid to ever make the Banzai Run down Third Street on his bicycle."

I glance at Manny to see how he reacts to the Banzai. No one but me knows about Manny's close call. His face has no expression.

So Nino-'n-Smitty take turns doing the gory details about the tale of Cesar Aguilar and the final Banzai Run. All about how he made it all the way to the bottom of the Run and was almost through the last intersection and home free when this tractor pulled in front of him. It was hauling a trailer with a big backhoe with the blade sticking up in the back like some giant stinger. Cesar twisted his bike sideways and missed the tractor. And he missed the trailer. And he just about missed the blade, except he didn't duck low enough.

They never found his head.

Nino-'n-Smitty each has a different story about what happened after that. Nino tells how Cesar wandered around looking for that head and got revenge on anyone he thought might have stole it. Smitty says how that head popped up in weird places like some poor kid's refrigerator, or on some girl's pillow and when she pulls back the covers there's no body.

So, if a tale is different according to whatever guy tells it, then who does it belong to? All of us? None of us? Most like, this is Cesar's tale.

After his tale is all told, we just lie inside our bags and stare up at all the stars, listening to the pounding of the waves, and once in a while staring at that dark bus. We huddle up against the dune for shelter against the wind. I'm naked inside my bag 'cause I can't stand that sandy, salty itching no more.

"Hey," Manny whispers.

"What?"

"Which would be worse, finding Cesar's head in your sleeping bag or hearing his footsteps creeping at you in the sand?"

That's when I can tell he's finally okay about the Banzai.

"No contest," I say. "I'd rather find the head."

"What if it's all decayed with rotted teeth grinning at you?"

"I'd still pick the head."

"Why?"

"'Cause it ain't got legs to chase me."

Nino-'n-Smitty bust up laughing. But I'm mostly glad to hear Manny laughing, too.

I should have known better than to get them going. They both jump up, grab my bag, zip me inside, drag me over the sand dune, and carry me, my butt bouncing on the sand, for what seems like forever. Even through the bag I feel the cold wind.

By the time I get my head out of the bag they're long gone back to camp. I'm all the way at the rocks at the far end of the cove. I can just picture them back at the fire, having their stupid laugh, just waiting for me to come hopping back. So I curl up inside the bag like it's some kind of shell and try to get some z's. My flashlight is in the bag, and I turn that on and burrow to the bottom. The wind makes all kinds of creepy sounds that could be a headless body creeping along the sand. It's hard breathing in the closed-in space of the bag.

I guess I fall asleep, 'cause I'm waking up. I poke my head out, and the night is lit by a full moon hanging over the water. Something woke me, but I can't figure what. Everything is quiet. The wind has died down, and it's almost warm. But it's not quiet after all. There's the soft sound of toes slapping in the water.

I bury my head back inside.

A weird sea kind of smell seeps into the bag. It's not like any sea smell I've ever whiffed in all the times I been down there. I poke my head out of the bag.

I sit up.

I feel dizzy like my whole life has gone crazy, but maybe the old hippies slipped me some acid or something. The sand all along the edge of the water is alive. It's a squirming, day-glo silver snake. I stand up, the still air clinging to me. The full moon cuts a silver line across the water.

I walk along that squirming, glowing edge.

It's grunion.

I creep through so I don't squish none, the waves lapping at me. Grunion are flopping against my legs, dancing around my feet, nuzzling in the sand. I smell their dance, their eggs.

I feel someone behind me.

I turn.

It's the girl from the bus, standing at the edge of the wet sand. She walks down and stands beside me. We hold hands. She stands almost a head taller, but it's no big deal. We walk along in that squirming mess. The sand oozes between our toes.

She leads me back to my bag without saying nothing.

We lie like spoons, but it's nothing to do with the sounds that come from my mom's end of the trailer when she's got a prospect. That's not what it's about at all. The feel of her body, of the thin bones. And her smell like the grunion, only sweeter. Her soft breath sounding like if the ocean could whisper.

In the morning, I wake up alone.

The sky is just turning pink. The bus is gone. So are the grunion.

CHAPTER TWENTY-TWO

EXCALIBUR

Charley and me are digging through the junk in Mrs. Elliot's backyard. The collectibles. There's not much out here worth passing off as Leguin's, but I can't afford to go inside. I'm just sort of kicking around some old farm tools when my shoe snags on a piece of metal.

"Over here, Charley." This is no farm tool.

He hobbles over. He's getting longer. When was the last time I carried him? It was the night Leguin caught him. We've sort of gone our own ways this summer.

I flip over a broke rake and there's a beat-up, rusty bike frame with some sweet curves. I toss junk right and left until I get it uncovered. It's an ancient Schwinn. My hands wrap around it, and I feel this power hum right through me kind of like grabbing an ungrounded cord. I reach down and pull, but it's snagged on something.

Charley stands beside me, just staring.

I grab that sucker tight, the rust flaking and biting my hands. I yank hard and the frame jumps out, pieces of a rake falling off. I lift it over my head, feeling just like Arthur when he pulled out that sword, and I carry it to Mrs. Elliot's back door, my heart pounding the whole time.

"Mrs. Elliot," I call through the screen.

"So you've found something." She opens the screen and grins down at me. "What is it this time?" She wipes her hands on the apron that covers the square-dancing skirts. She sees the bike frame, and that grin fades to a tight line. "So, you found something special."

We just stand staring at each other until I feel Charley tugging on my shirt.

"Nothing special," I finally say. "Just an old rusty bike frame I thought I could fix. Needs a lot of work, though. I might go ten bucks."

She just stands there with that grim look.

"Okay, thirteen," I say.

"Not for sale," she says.

It don't make sense, her doing a hard sell on an old bike frame. It makes even less sense that I need it with all my money troubles from Buying Time. "Fifteen. That's as high as I can go . . ."

"You didn't hear me," she says. "It's not for sale."

I study her face. She means it.

"Look, if this has to do with my tab, I'll pay cash." I dig in my pockets.

"This has nothing to do with money," she says.

"Everything has to do with money."

"You don't believe that any more than I do, RJ."

What can I say?

She sighs.

"You don't know about that bike," she says.

So here comes the family story. Maybe there's some hope for her selling it, after all. She only does the family number to jack up a price.

"This is a sad story about a wonderful boy. It happened twelve years ago. Little Cesar, we call him."

Cesar . . . the Banzai Run . . .

"Cesar Aguilar." I drop the bike frame. "I already know that story."

"No," she says. "No one really knows the story. Little Cesar is my nephew. You remind me of him, RJ."

"I know all about the Banzai Run."

"You know he was forced into it?"

I don't answer. That isn't part of the legend.

"There's a . . . a gang of hoodlums have a hideout up in the hills."

"The Blackjacks," I say.

"You know them?"

"Yeah, I know them."

"Yes, of course you do. Everyone knows the Blackjacks. They wouldn't leave little Cesar alone."

"You're saying they . . . like, made Cesar do the Run? Then it's like they killed him."

"Killed? Little Cesar wasn't killed."

"Then how . . ."

"Badly, badly hurt. But not killed. He lives in Salinas with his mother. Leaving this valley was the only way she could free him."

"Mrs. Elliot." I hold the frame up to her. "I need it."

"It's not for sale." She uses her apron to wipe her cheeks.

"I will not have that on my conscience. But if you need it that badly, take it."

There's nothing more to say. I turn and walk away. It's not easy hauling that frame with Charley hanging on my back. I stop and he drops off.

"This ain't working no more. You got to walk."

"I know," he says.

"When I rebuild this bike, you can have the Stingray."

He nods.

I must be nuts making a big deal out of this old frame, but there's all this stuff bouncing around in my head . . . *Buying Time, the Old Tumbler, the Banzai Run, the Blackjacks, Leguin, Theresa, the root cellar, little Cesar* . . . and it feels like it's all coming together, somehow, in this bike frame.

CHAPTER TWENTY-THREE

FRECKLES

I'm gliding in these ever-increasing squares on the streets around the trailer park, the Old Tumbler in the cage on my Stingray handlebars. I'm not really sure just how you train these pigeons to home. Maybe it's just an instinct, but I figure it won't hurt to give him a sort of tour.

Three girls are walking along the sidewalk away from me, toward one of the houses in the little tract by the elementary. Two are blondes wobbling on wedges. Even from behind. Especially from behind. I recognize the middle girl, and my heart slips out of whack. I take deep breaths. It's never a good idea. Never. To sneak up on a gaggle of girls by yourself. But here I am gliding up next to them.

"Hey."

They stop and turn. I don't remember the names of the two fake blondes who are trying to look sixteen. They got that puffy hair, lots of makeup, and shoulder pads in their blouses. They look like they got some other pads, too. I mean, real titties never look like that. Theresa still has the razor-cut bangs and straight brown hair, but now there's reddish streaks from the sun. Her skin is a light olive, with summer freckles along the cheeks, not covered by makeup. And there's definitely no padding under that peasant blouse.

People outside the valley might think it weird, that those two wannabe discos would be hanging out with Theresa. But she has this friendly yet *don't mess with me* attitude that makes other girls want to be her friend, even if she is different. What I do wonder is why she would hang with them. But here, if you're going to a party, which is what they look like, you're pretty much stuck with what you got for friends.

"Look, Teetee, it's RJ," the one on the right says, elbowing Theresa. "And he's blushing."

"Oh my God . . ." the left side girl says. "He has something in that cage on his handlebars."

"It's a pigeon," I say. I don't even know why I bother to answer.

"You really are weird," the right one says.

"Yeah, is this some freaky thing like your brother's toe shows?"

"Leave his brother out of this," Theresa says.

"The other boys shoot those things," the right side girl says. "Rats on wings, my brother calls them. And you got one in a cage."

"I suppose it's got a broken wing or something and you want to fix it," the other one says in a fake voice.

"No. It's kind of old, but it's okay," I say. "Flies real good. It tumbles, but . . ."

This makes them laugh. Man, I sound stupid.

"You guys go on ahead, and I'll catch up," Theresa says.

"Ooohhh," they say as they wobble away.

"They call you Teetee?" I tease.

But she don't smile back. She glares at me.

"Sometimes, when I dream . . ." Her voice is quiet and flat. "I'm soaring through the clouds. I can feel the breeze, but it's completely silent. I am gliding above . . ." She waves across the fields and buildings and the hills. "All this."

"Yeah," I say. "I . . ."

That glare shuts me up.

"And you have a creature that can soar like that. And you put it in a cage."

"No, it's not like that . . ."

"If I could fly, and you put me in a cage, I would die." She turns. "The other boys are kinder when they shoot them."

She walks away.

"Theresa!" I push off from the curb, but the cage has shifted, and the bike falls over, the cage door flying open. If the Old Tumbler escapes out here, this soon, I don't know if he could survive, much less find his way home.

Theresa looks back.

The Old Tumbler checks out the opening. I could lift him out, toss him flying, point up at him. Show him off . . . But if I do, he might fly away and be gone forever and ever. I shove him back in and latch the door.

Nothing I can do but watch her turn and walk away.

I wrestle the cage back between the handlebars and ride home. Charley is waiting for me as I glide around back.

"Today is it," I say.

"What?" Charley asks.

"Tumbling."

I lean the Stingray up against a post of the coop. What does

Theresa know about flying? This coop is all quality redwood I bought from the lumberyard. I know I should have saved the bucks for Buying Time, but I can make money selling the baby birds, and that coop will help me close the deal. It's open in front with chicken wire. It has a big door in front so I can reach in to clean it out or when I just want to grab the birds. But the best part is this little pigeon door in the middle of the big door.

But does Theresa care about any of this?

Sure, it's been closed so far because I can't risk them flying away forever. But after the birds have made it their home, I can pull it down and it'll make like a perch. Then they can come and go whenever they want, using the little door as a launching pad.

Charley just watches as I get the stepladder. I built that coop on stilts so no cats could snag the birds. How long do you keep them locked in? It's been almost two weeks. Anyway, the Old Tumbler isn't going anywhere with his Amazing Grace sitting back in the nesting box with an egg.

What does Theresa know about real flying?

All the sibs watch me from the screened porch of the trailer. They've been waiting for this ever since I first started pounding away on the wood.

So I'm leading a regular pilgrimage out to the fields. I'm first, the Old Tumbler tucked in my right hand. Then there's Charley hobbling along without help. Amy lugs her boneless cat, Peabody, over her shoulder. The twins are right behind her. Mom leads Peanut by the hand.

I check out the sky for hawks. I should make some sort of speech, but I can't think what to say that wouldn't sound stupid next to what he's about to do, so I just toss him. The

Old Tumbler flies straight for the only cloud in the sky. He's taking off for good. What will I tell the old man?

Then he comes to that full stop. And he starts the slide. Halfway down he goes into the tumble. I take my eyes off him just long enough to judge the reaction. Not as great as I hoped, but he's got their attention.

"Well?" I ask.

"Would've been neat if he *hadn't* made it," Amy says, rubbing Peabody under the chin. Even Peabody looks just barely interested. "Do they ever not make it?"

I pretend I don't hear her. "What did you think, Mom?"

"Interesting, dear." She's wearing her black-and-white waitress uniform, which always makes me sad. "I've got to get to work now."

"What's wrong with that bird?" Stevie asks.

"Yeah," Suzy adds, "you ought to get your money back. It's . . . funny."

About the only one who appreciates is Charley. He's still standing there after the others are long gone.

CHAPTER TWENTY-FOUR
DEFECTIVE

The Old Tumbler is checking me out from that little launching pad door I leave open most of the time now. He's bobbing his head from one side to the other to get a view from both eyes. The Schwinn parts lie on an old blanket almost underneath the coop. It's about the only spot where there's some shade. It'll hit a hundred for the third day in a row. Charley sits on the edge of a cinder block, watching me with that blank expression that drives a lot of guys nuts.

"Time to put this sucker together," I say.

The Old Tumbler coos.

I run my hands over that bike frame. Three coats of primer and four coats of gunmetal gray. Sanded smooth after each coat. I helped Mr. Olson restock at Big O's Hardware and Feed in exchange for the paint and for my promise it won't be for graffiti.

It takes forever to pull out the pedals, which are rusted into the frame. I sand and oil and repack them.

Amazing Grace coos from inside one of the nesting boxes. She's been sitting on that egg a long time and she means business. The Old Tumbler coos back at her from the launching pad, but he don't take flight.

I bolt on the wheels. The chain is brand-new from Mike's Bike Shop.

The funky smell of the coop just sort of simmers in that heat. A redwood, straw, feathers, and bird shit kind of smell. I love the smell of that coop.

No fenders. This bike is streamlined.

The swamp cooler fan rattles and shimmies in the trailer window. It's propped up on a pair of two-by-fours that could split any day. The whole side of the trailer hums.

All that's left that I need for this bike is the handlebars. I stand up, staring at that poor headless thing. It's not like I haven't been looking. You just don't rush into something like that.

I go into the bathroom and scrub off the grease.

"RJ! RJ!" Charley calls from out back.

I run out and Charley is hopping up and down, pointing at the coop. I go over and look inside. There's this squeaking noise coming from inside the nesting box. I open the big door. The Old Tumbler bobs his head back and forth and rubs his beak against the floor and puffs out his chest. I lean inside the coop and peek in the nesting box. The thing inside is all wet, with an oversized head, bug eyes, and not one feather.

Charley keeps tugging at my shirt.

"Jeez, Charley, I won't get any money off that thing unless it's in a freak show."

Charley tries to crawl over my back, so I let him look.

The Old Tumbler coos like crazy.

"That's enough, Charley. Give them some privacy."

I close the big door. He's still staring as I turn and walk away. Maybe he's thinking if he can't run, maybe he can fly.

I head for Leguin's, just cruising on the Stingray over asphalt shimmering with heat waves, cruising like some cholo lowrider. He'll want to hear the bad news about the baby bird. Little kids are playing on the squeaky dead grass of the hills. They're shouting just to hear their voices skipping through the hot air like a mean fastball, and I wish I was there, but I won't ever be that age again.

Buying Time has to end somewhere, so why don't I just lay it all out to the old man? Maybe he'd even give me something to take to the Blackjacks. No, that wouldn't be his style. He'd say something grown-up like *You must go to the police.* He'd say something lame that would get us dead. Or worse, he'd stare at me with a feel-sorry look.

Sparklers left over from the Fourth stick out of my pocket and brush against my back as I pedal.

What if Leguin decided to do something about the Blackjacks himself? He's too weak to make a stand against them, but somehow he'd have his weapons. One could be Roxanne. One could be me.

The thought hits me so hard I stop the bike and sit down by the side of the road. *What if he's already using me and I don't even know it?*

I sit there long enough to feel the pounding heat give way to an evening breeze sliding across the dry grass. Getting up and heading for that old man's house is one of the hardest things I ever did.

I don't much remember the ride or stopping at A&W, but

here I am hopping up the steps of Leguin's house with a bag of burgers and fries. I stare through the screen and see him lying on the couch.

"Are you dead or are you asleep?"

"I can't seem to manage either one." A washcloth covers his eyes.

"Well, if you're planning to die, don't count on me sticking around."

He lifts up a corner of the washcloth and stares out at me. He scowls at the greasy bag, but I figure even he can do better than rice and bananas.

"Are you going to stand out there all evening?"

I step inside. When he's lying down, he's so small and shriveled that it looks like that couch has swallowed him whole. There's only one glass on the coffee table. The bottle of sherry is nearly empty.

I take the bag in the kitchen and pour the fries on a couple of plates. He won't eat unless it's on a plate. The cheeseburgers are lukewarm and soggy. I pour my soda into one of the crystal glasses. The plan about sneaking back at night and stealing the crystal feels easier than ever, except that I still can't do it.

He's fighting the couch, trying to get up as I put the plates on the coffee table. I lift him so he can sit on the edge, and he's so light that he feels hollow. He really does look like a vampire, that hunched-over creature with the hooked nose and creepy fingers.

"The tumbler hatched."

"You don't sound very pleased at this particular nativity."

He gums a fry.

"Well, I seen a few things get born, and I know all

about how they can look ugly coming out, but that baby is defective."

He snorts so hard it sounds like he sucked a fry up his nose. I get him a glass of water and he's still snorting. He waves the water away and downs some sherry.

"Child, it is supposed to look that way," he wheezes.

"I knew that."

We eat without talking except for when he laughs and snorts, remembering what I said. I don't like being laughed at, so maybe I'll tell him a story to get it out of his head.

"I got a tale."

He pushes his plate away and leans back into the sofa.

Maybe it's the idea of getting born defective that has me telling this story, or maybe it's just the need for cash.

The Tale of Charley's Toes and Their Greater Purpose

My all-time most favorite business was selling toes. Not my own, of course. I sold my brother Charley's toes. A quarter to see four, a half dollar to see all seven to eight and a half, depending on how you read his toe lines. And a buck for the big toe show for an audience of three or more. A bargain. His toes put on a good show. Charley didn't mind. At least, he never said he did. He even let me make them up special, like when I painted them green for the St. Patrick's Day toe show. What a great draw it would've been if I could've painted little faces, or maybe even Christmas trees, on his toenails. Except he didn't have no toenails. Of course, if he had, there wouldn't have been a show in the first place. Life's got its twists like that. There were operations to fix his toes. Some even helped. Then Mom lost her insurance about the same time a doctor botched one up and ruined my brother for walking and it took another operation just to get him back to normal—his normal, not ours. Uncle Ted, who belongs to Amy, always said things like, "God never errs, boys. There must be some greater purpose to Charley's toes!" I always hated when he'd say that 'cause for a week after that Charley, whenever he'd see me, he'd wiggle his sorry excuses for toes with that smirk on his face, just knowing they were signed up for some Greater Purpose.

Well, the last toe show began in sixth grade with this brand-new kid in the valley, Mike Dudley, who everyone called Milk Dud. I started giving him the usual line about my brother's toes. You know, sort of catching his interest, building him to the clincher, when I'd offer to show him—for a small fee. You probably know all about that, what with being in the insurance racket.

Anyway, I got POed when Dud started laughing. I didn't allow laughing at Charley's toes. That was always the number one rule at any toe show. But Dud said he wasn't laughing at his toes. He was laughing 'cause his sister had a whole foot that was weird and it would outgross my brother's toes anytime, anyplace. Well, no way, Jose. We got a bet going, and things got out of hand. Seeing as it was near Halloween, we set the contest for Debby Welsh's Halloween party.

I figured I'd better get Charley a bitchin' pair of new sneakers for his show. The A-number-one rule any time we went for shoes was to pick out a young, cute saleslady. So we sat down and the saleslady came over, not suspecting nothing. She got out that metal thing with the slides on it and pulled up a stool in front of Charley. She had these big brown eyes and was hands down the cutest and youngest shoe lady we'd ever had. Charley stuck a foot out and she began to unlace it as I tried hard not to snicker. Charley just stared at her with that blank look of his. Finally, she got that shoe off, wads of TP dropping out, and she frowned. She rolled her big browns up at Charley and he smiled that sweet smile and so she just pulled his socks on down.

Usually, the shoe ladies tried to hide their reaction. That never worked, of course. Sometimes they'd say something like Oh God! One thing they always did was drop Charley's foot like they thought they'd catch some weird disease. But this shoe lady, she forgot to even drop the foot. She just sat there dripping tears on it for the longest time. Charley smiled and watched those pretty little hands cradling his foot.

Anyway, Charley went to that party as an angel, and the halo my mom made gave it just the right touch. I went as a devil. When Milk Dud arrived, he played their entrance for all it was worth. He flipped aside the cape of his Dracula costume, which fit his personality perfect, and waved his sister in. She stood staring at us, a Little Bo Peep all the way from the pretty little dress to that shepherd's stick. She was a couple months older than my brother, even though they were both in the second grade. She had long wavy hair even blonder than my brother's, huge green eyes, and a sweet heart-shaped face. She stepped slowly into the room. Man, the feet! Plastic shiny shoes with lacy ankle socks. The right shoe was twice as big as the left.

Charley just patted me on the back and said he'd give it his best shot. What a gutsy kid. Guys shouted side bets all around. And the odds all went to Lisa after they eyeballed her shoes. Lisa went first. She sat down, sniffling the whole time. First she inched off her little left shoe and her little left sock. The audience gasped as out popped the prettiest, most perfect foot anyone had ever seen. Dud was sharp, playing the contrast angle like that. Her lower lip sort of shook as she unlaced that oversized right shoe. Well, as she unrolled that lacy sock, I fell back in my seat. The crowd gasped. There was no way, Jose, that Charley could match that. A couple girls made quick exits.

But Charley, he was no quitter. He sat down real slow, cracked his knuckles, and began unwinding the plaid laces. But interest had already faded. Half the guys wandered away before he even had that first shoe unlaced. It was too bad, really. That was the all-time best show he'd ever given. By the time he reached the finale, the room was practically empty except for the judges, who were already arguing over who bet what.

That's when it happened. Lisa hobbled over to Charley and threw her arms around his neck, kissing him on the forehead, on the cheek, on the lips, and knocking his halo all crooked. Charley took it pretty good, that being the first time he'd been kissed by a girl and all.

That was a tough year for me, what with Charley strutting around the house wiggling those digits at me with that expression like there was some Greater Purpose to it all. Asking me if I had a girlfriend yet. Saying how he preferred older women.

CHAPTER TWENTY-FIVE

HALF A SISTER

Leguin lies with his head back, his breath raspy. Toe Dough is one of my favorite tales, but it just put him to sleep like he was one of the sibs. I could walk out right now with anything I feel like. I rise, holding the crystal glasses, and edge toward the front door.

"Where are you going with that crystal?" He stares at me through half-open lids, and I know he wasn't asleep. Had it been a trick?

"I . . . I was taking them out to the kitchen to clean up."

"Leave it." He leans forward. "Sit down."

I should say something to take his mind off the crystal. "What was Roxanne doing here? I mean, you said she'd been here three times. I think . . . I think you owe me some explaining."

"I do not," he says.

"I've been doing chores and telling you all these lame stories, most of them I haven't told to nobody, and you say you don't owe me? Worse, I've been . . . been . . ."

"Yes?" He studies me and it's almost like he knows about the Blackjacks. But how could he?

"Nothing." I look away.

"How old were you when your father died?" he asks.

"What does that . . . Three. I was three."

"How did he die?"

"War killed him."

"But he wasn't in combat at the time?"

"War can do that. Kill you after. But I've seen your photo in there, so I figure you know all about what war can do."

"Indeed. How old was Roxanne?"

"When my dad died? Five, maybe six, I guess. But what does that—"

"Your father is also Roxanne's father."

I stare at the old man's face, at the melting eyes. How could he even know this? She told him. Was she telling the truth? I see back through my life at all the mean things Roxanne done to me, at all the hateful things her mom said. This hate went even deeper than just some jealousy between our moms. Way deeper.

"RJ . . ."

"Just shut up. Okay? Just . . . let me think."

And then all the weird comments people made to me over the years make sense . . .

And then there's Mom's tale of that hate between our families. Sometimes a lie is not what is twisted around inside a tale, but what lurks outside. That's the worst kind of lie. The kind Mom made to me all these years.

"That means . . ." One second Roxanne is just this freakish girl, and the next she's my half a sister. I try and squeeze this idea into my world, but I can't. That one little word, "sister," changes everything. "I gotta go."

"Wait."

I stop at the door, staring out the screen at the sky that's doing its fade. But I don't turn around.

"Look out here," I say. "What did you call this time?"

"*L'heure bleue,*" he whispers. "The blue hour."

"People think a kid don't remember that far back, but I do. Lying in bed waiting for him to come sing me to sleep. Holding a kite and wanting him to wrap his arms around me and grab the string so we'd share that feel of the wind tugging on it."

My hand brushes the sparkler in my pocket. "Today is the fourteenth."

"Yes. Bastille Day," he says.

"I brought you a surprise."

I step out on the dirt drive where he can see me through the open front door. I hold up the sparkler and light it and hold it over my head like the Statue of Liberty.

"*Vive la France!*" he shouts.

The sparks dance in the twilight, and I don't even care if the whole world catches fire. But the world don't burn and the sparkler fizzles. I stomp it out in the dirt, climb back up the steps, and plop in my chair.

"Thank you," he says.

"No problem," I say.

We sit a long time listening to the quiet.

"RJ, if Roxanne is in peril, then there is only one person who can help. There is only one person who cares."

"You think I should care?" I stand. "If she's half a sister, it also means she's half a *not* sister, too. And that *not* half has been all she's ever shown me. So now I'm supposed to take care of her, too? She's the older one. Where was she all this time?"

He don't answer.

It's getting dark outside and we haven't lit candles, so the house is crawling in shadows as I turn and leave without looking back.

I'm halfway up the hill behind the barn when it hits me that the old man never really did answer my question about what Roxanne had been doing there. Or did he, and I just didn't hear it?

I sit near the top of the hill overlooking the old man's house. The moon is just rising above Big Mama. The sky is lighter shades of purple, but the house is in shadow. A flicker of candlelight moves against the living room window. The screen door opens. The old man hobbles out without his cane, carrying a candle in one hand and something that looks like a book or bag in the other. He creeps around the outbuildings to the root cellar door. No way he could lift that door, but he does. He stops and looks around. I hold my breath as he stares up the hill to where I'm sitting. I don't move, don't breathe. He stays like that for a minute and then turns back to the cellar. He steps down inside, pulling the door shut over him.

Roxanne warned me not to come here no more. I figured she was warning me about Leguin, and maybe she was. But maybe she was really warning me against something else. Down in that cellar.

But what about Roxanne? If she didn't run away and she's not in that cellar, then where is she? If I cross out Leguin, her mom, a boyfriend, and even herself as suspects, who's left? The Blackjacks.

Man, it's crazy I didn't think of them first thing. Maybe the whole reason she first went to Leguin was that the Blackjacks had sent her on a task, just like me. And if she had failed, they would have punished her. What would they have done to her?

Purgatory.

The word hits me hard, like someone slapped me upside the head with it.

Purgatory.

The Blackjacks might have her locked up in that old water tank. But if I go to the sheriff's and if they even believe me enough to check it out, the Blackjacks will get so much warning that they could do anything to her long before help arrived.

Why should I care? Why should I risk my life for someone who treated me like dirt? I lie back, listening to the summer night sounds, building up the nerve to sneak up Dead Man's Gorge because I got no other choice. She's my half a sister.

CHAPTER TWENTY-SIX

PURGATORY

I stash my bike behind a boulder and crawl up on the trail to Dead Man's Gorge. Half a moon lights the path so I don't use the flashlight I got shoved in my back pocket. When the ripply clouds cover the moon, I creep forward. When the moon slides out again, I stop. Check out the trail ahead. Then creep ahead when it's dark.

My shoe slips off the path, rocks clicking down the hill, and it's like the noise is bouncing all over the valley. I lie against the side of the hill, trying not to breathe so loud. Where's the Blackjacks' lookout? They got to have at least one. I see a big bend in the trail just ahead, and I know that as soon as I round it, I'll see that creepy old oak like a big shadow in the night.

I must be almost over purgatory by now. The moon peeks out and there's that hump just ten yards below the trail, with that yellow hatch sticking out of the rocks. I've stopped right over it, like it was some kind of instinct. If they got Roxanne, she's in there. But that tank is out in the open and there's nowhere for a guy to hide. I scope out the territory. No one. I wait for cloud cover and I slide down the rocks on my Chucks. I land right on top of the hatch and hang on. The moon pops out and it feels like all that light is aimed right at me.

There's no lock, just this metal bar slid through a hole in the latch and a hole in the frame. Nothing could get out with that bar slid in like that. I shove the bar out and it makes a rusty scraping sound that rattles up and down the tank and echoes back even louder. I drop the bar beside the tank and listen for what's inside.

Nothing.

My arms shake as I grab the hatch and pull, figuring it'll creek and groan, but it lifts silently. The darkness slides up at me.

"Anyone in there?"

I didn't know you were chick-en . . . Roxanne's voice whispers inside my head, and I remember back to that root cellar. But it takes a minute for my breath to come back.

I take the flashlight and lean over and drop my arm as far down into the blackness as I can, so the light won't show up above when I flick it on. What if something down there grabs my hand?

I push the switch. No light. I shake it. It flickers on, then off before I can see anything. Then it comes on dim. The batteries must be going out. I lean over and stick my head inside and wave the light. Somehow, the tank looks bigger from the inside. The round sides make it look like the belly of some beast. Candy wrappers and crumpled cigarette packs litter the floor. But there's no one in there.

I pull back out, sucking in the clean night air.

Wait. There was something. Some kind of writing on the peeling yellow paint. Or had I imagined it? I stick my head in again, shaking the flashlight until it comes on. Something like purple paint, or maybe just scrapes, against the far wall. It's for sure letters, though I can't see from up here what they say.

I pull back out and suck air.

There's no way I'm going down there. No way.

It won't take but a minute to drop down, crawl over, read the letters, crawl back, and pull myself out. My chest thumps just thinking about it.

No way I'm going down in there.

I can't come this far and not find out. I check the hatch lid. It's all the way open, and it's so heavy there's no way it could close by accident. So what could happen? Wouldn't take more than a minute. Just one minute.

No way.

I lie on my stomach, turn, and drop my legs through the opening down into the blackness. What the hell am I doing? My feet dangle inside like floating next to my boogie board with that whole creepy sea under me and a shark or something just waiting to come floating up and swallow me. I can still pull out.

But I drop inside.

The flashlight shakes in my hand and the light flickers. I can do this in one minute. Thirty seconds if I hustle. I crawl across the tank. The floor is wet, slimy. My hand slips on a sticky wrapper.

The flashlight goes out. A faint moonlight from the hatch. I shake the light. Nothing. The blackness starts to close around me. Breathe deep.

Deeper.

Deeper. Slow and steady and deep. I shake the flashlight hard and there's a glow. I crawl to the end and aim it at the wall. It's purplish paint.

Foxy Roxy purple.

It's toenail polish.

It's too smeared to read. *Help* . . . *hell* . . . I don't need to read it to know what it means.

The light goes out. Gone out for good.

She had written it with toenail polish. Foxy Roxy purple.

I crawl back toward the hatch.

A thud against the top of the tank.

Kaablllaaaammmmm! It's the loudest sound I ever heard in my whole life.

Blackness. Total blackness.

The sound of a bolt sliding through metal.

CHAPTER TWENTY-SEVEN

LADY FINGER

The world is black.

How long have I been here? Not long in for real time. But it feels like forever.

Why didn't I think to bring that bolt with me?

A sound rasps through the walls of the water tank like a heavy breather. My head spins in the dark, and the whole side of the tank is going in and out, in and out under my hand, like I'm inside something alive. I hold my breath so I can hear better. The breathing sound stops. I exhale and the water tank does, too. It's just my echo.

Chick-en . . . chick-en . . .

Where did that come from?

Outside? No . . .

Inside the tank? No.

Inside. Inside my head. That's where I am. That's where she is now, inside my head. That's where she's standing, inside my head. Black hair around her shoulders. Drops of rainwater hanging on the ends of fake lashes around black, black eyes. That wet tee. A smell oozing from her. Not a bottled-up smell, all her . . . And her toes in rainbow surfer sandals.

She reaches out and grabs my hand. She's leading me down . . . down a long black spiral . . .

Ka-blang! I'm in that root cellar again. *I can't believe you fell for that.* Her whisper bouncing all around the root cellar stones . . . all around this metal tank . . . all around my skull . . .

The smell of the old stone of that root cellar all over again . . . I'm rocking back and forth, back and forth . . . my butt floating off the ground . . . Then I hear it again, from outside the cellar . . . a foot dragging in the mud . . . a flashlight beam blinding me . . . a hand coming out of the darkness . . . like a claw . . .

Only this time it's not the old man. It's Roxanne grabbing my hand, yanking me out of the cellar.

She's pulling me deeper down that black spiral . . .

I'm back at Father Speckler's class, lying in that coat closet in the dark . . . a little crack of light under the door . . . hard to breathe . . . Father Speckler shouting, "All God's children!"

Then she's leading me deeper.

The door of a trailer . . . YOURE HOOSTE. Smell of booze and rotten food . . . a sicker smell under that. She's opening the trailer door. I'm not going in there. I'm following little round pictures of pilgrims marching around the inside of Mr. Sanders's trailer . . . that smell . . . a thing lying against the bed . . . the trailer door, with its fresh air and light somewhere far, far, far behind me . . . the thing is half off the bed like it's saying good-night prayers . . .

Not that not that not that . . .

I break out of Roxanne's hold . . .

I'm back in the water tank. It's now again. Roxanne's gone.
But she was in here. Not with me. Before.

Alone.

I crawl to the hatch, my hand slipping against something
slimy on the floor. I'm under it now. My head whacks metal
as I stand up. There are a couple holes where the metal has
rusted. I put my nose up next to them.

Who's in there?

Did that come from inside my head? No. A voice outside.

"Who's in there?"

I know that voice.

"Bobby? Bobby Martin?" I suck air.

"Well, if it ain't RJ. I've sorta been expecting you."

"Open the hatch, Bobby."

Silence.

"Bobby, open the hatch!"

"I can't do that."

"Sure you can. Just slide out that bolt."

"You know what I mean."

"You're the lookout?"

"Yeah."

"Guess that's lucky for me." I try and laugh.

Silence.

"Open the hatch, Bobby."

"No way."

"No one has to know," I say.

"He'd know."

A longer silence.

"Remember . . ." Bobby's voice sounds faraway. ". . . when

we used to take insects and lizards and put 'em in a can and blow 'em all to hell with a Lady Finger?"

I stare at pinpricks of light. "Bobby, open the hatch. Please."

"Thought I'd lost you. But where would you go?" He laughs. "Remember that *crraaack* sound? I haven't done a tin can in a long time. Remember that smell afterward?"

"I remember. Why don't you just open the hatch, Bobby. Like for old times' sake, you know?" Breathe deep. Just stare at the little holes and focus on Bobby's words.

"Did you ever wonder, RJ, what it felt like in one of those tin cans?"

"No."

"Nah, you wouldn't. I knew you never liked doing that . . . Say, I bet an M-80 in this water tank would feel about the same to one of us as that tin can felt to one of them bugs."

"For God's sake, Bobby."

"God's sake? That's a good one. You know what Roxanne used to say? *Fer the love-a Gaawd.*"

Silence again.

Say something. Keep him here. Keep him talking.

"So, you're the lookout. That must be a tough job."

"Don't try none of your psycho stuff on me, RJ. Nothin' tough about this job. No one except you'd be lame enough to come up here at night. The Ace said that. He's been expecting you."

"You could let me out and I'd be down that hill so fast no one would know, not even him. I won't tell, Bobby."

"That was a nasty trick, RJ."

"Huh? What?"

"That was a nasty trick you pulled about those kittens."

"Kittens? . . . What . . . That was a long, long time ago, Bobby."

"Just let you go? You mean just like you did with them kittens? You told me to go for the Lady Fingers. You said you'd watch the kittens until I got back. You said we could blow them sky-high. Put a whole pack in there. And when I got back, you and the kittens was gone. That was low-down."

I don't answer.

"I really hated you for that. You know why?"

"No."

"'Cause you messed up my last chance."

"I couldn't let the kittens get blown up, Bobby. I couldn't."

"You don't see it, do you? You messed up my last chance to be good. Every time I'd catch something, I'd tell myself, this time I ain't gonna do it. This time I'm gonna be good. But . . . something . . . I don't know. I'd end up doing it again. But kittens, I knew I couldn't blow up kittens. But you. You had to steal them before I could even find out . . . I know they'd have been the . . . the limit . . . I know I couldn't have blown up kittens . . . and you screwed it all up."

"Bobby, I can't breathe."

"There are holes where it's rusted through. You're standing by one now."

"I can't BREATHE!"

"Take it slow. Slow, deep breaths . . . What did you do with them?"

"The kittens? Gave them away. Except one. My sister kept one."

"Yeah? Which one?"

"The black one."

"What did she name it?"

184

"Peabody."

"Peabody . . . You scared in there, RJ?"

"Yeah."

"Good."

"So are you, Bobby."

"Me? Yeah, me too. I been scared up here a whole long time. It's getting bad. Real bad."

"Bobby, listen. You can still change."

"Bull. You always thought you knew everything. The way you'd con people. Always getting your way. Always good with words. You think you can do it even now."

"I just want out."

"It's too late."

"No! No one even saw me. Just . . ."

"I ain't talking about you. Too late for her. Too late for the Blackjacks. Too late for all of us."

What's that even mean? Breathe. Dizzy. Just breathe.

"Bobby! You still there, Bobby?"

"Yeah."

"Let me out. Tell the cops about all that the Blackjacks done. They make deals. You're still only a kid."

"You think it's the cops that scare me? Man, I'd be dead so fast . . . Things is getting psycho. They never should have had a girl up here. Especially not a crazy girl. She thought she'd be some kind of twisted Wendy in a psychedelic Neverland. But the Blackjacks, they're way the other side of lost boys. It's so bad it's like . . . like the scared feeling is all around in the air. It's in the way guys stare at each other, like everyone's afraid someone else is gonna be the first to squeal."

"That's right, Bobby. *You* be the first. If you don't tell, someone else will."

"The Ace says it's all that old man's fault. Says it all started when he showed up. The younger dudes . . . the Deuces . . . don't come up here no more. And the Jokers, they don't bother to go after them."

"This is like the kittens all over . . . only now you got a second chance. You can be good this time."

No answer. Is he gone? Just focus on these tiny holes in the metal and suck air.

"Bobby . . . what happened to her? Where is she?"

The screech of the bolt sliding open. The hatch rising.

"Bobby?"

No answer.

I reach up at the night and grab the rim of the hatch. The blackness slides away as I pull myself out.

The most I can do is roll off the tank onto the rocks and gulp air, shaking.

Bobby is gone.

I lie staring up at the clouds and moon. The sky has this pink glow at the edge. Sunrise. The Blackjacks will be up soon. The cool air is sliding in, filling me up. My legs tremble. Can I walk? I claw my way up the rocks to the trail.

On my way home.

CHAPTER TWENTY-EIGHT

PEABODY

I climb out of the worst nightmare I ever had. The porch is dark and warm. There's a blanket over me, but I'm still in my clothes. This nightmare just won't break up and fade like it's supposed to . . . *Roxanne . . . the Blackjacks . . . purgatory . . .* Sunlight slants through a crack in the blinds. It must be afternoon. It wasn't a nightmare. It all happened. A sick flip in my stomach. It's all happening. The sleep had just been a hard, black nothing in between the for real nightmare.

"You sick?" Mom stands at the door from the trailer to the porch. She's wearing a blue paisley muumuu covered by her bead necklaces. She circles the room flicking open the blinds and then walks over and sits on the edge of the bed and touches my forehead.

"No fever. What's going on? Is it that Theresa? Is there something you want to talk about? You know, you'll have your growth spurt and outgrow her one of these days. Your dad was tall. And look at me."

"Nothing like that. Anyway, right now I don't feel like I got any growth left in me."

Her fingers work the plastic beads like a rosary.

Does she know Roxanne is my half a sister? Sure she knows. That's what that hate thing between her and Roxanne's mom is really all about. But how could she keep that from me?

"Is this something you got to talk out with a man? I've done my best, but maybe there's some things . . ."

"You've been teaching me all about *that* for a whole long time already."

There's hurt in her eyes and there's something inside me that's glad she hurts.

"You should have told me Roxanne was my sister."

"Half sister."

She chews on the end of her thick hair. When she does that, she almost looks like a little girl. Except for the gray streaks. She don't do colors in her hair since she gave up prospects. I won't think about them.

"Do you wish my dad was still alive?"

The only sound is the *click-click* of her beads.

"Every day."

"But if Dad was alive, then Amy and Charley and the twins and Peanut, they wouldn't be here."

"I'd like to think your father and I could still have had them."

"No. Heredity don't work that way. Wishing Dad back is the same as wishing them dead."

Click. Click.

"If we had been enough for him," I say, "then he wouldn't have done what he did."

"You can't think like that."

"Sure I can. I just did."

I lie against the beads as she runs her hand through my hair, the nightmare fading in her flowery smell.

"I got to get ready for work, Kiddo. Got the swing tonight." She grabs my face in her hands, lifting me away from her, and stares down at me. "I can't make it without you. I'm counting on you."

Then she walks out on me.

I put on my shoes and step out the screen door. The coop shimmers in the heat. The flying door is open. I've been letting the birds come and go when they want. A small lump lies in the dirt in front of the coop. The baby bird's head is hanging by stringy red things to the body. Ants are crawling inside. The neck is the only thing chewed. No coyotes done this 'cause the only tracks in that dry dirt are the little prints of a cat. Peabody done this. It's not the loss of income that gets me. I could maybe see it if that cat ate the bird. It's the thought of Peabody killing just for the fun of it that frosts my ass. I wrap the bird in a rag. Then I take the Old Tumbler out of the coop and put him in the portable. Amazing Grace won't leave her box, so I just let her be.

"Where you taking him?" Charley watches me from the porch shade.

"To a funeral. Want to come?"

"I don't like funerals."

I turn and study his face. "What do you know about funerals?"

He shrugs. "It's gonna rain, anyway."

"Rain? Man, it's ninety degrees out here. Hasn't rained all summer. What do you know?" I pick up the portable in one hand and the dead bird in the other and squeeze through the back fence and wander out onto the fields.

Charley don't follow.

I bury the baby deep so no creatures will dig it up. It feels lame saying words over a dead bird, so I don't. A warm drizzle hits my face, big slow drops that just plop on the dust, leaving this funky dirt smell. I pull out Old Tumbler and fling him into the sky. He's got the real eulogy.

He flies clear out of sight and I don't blame him if he keeps going, but he don't. He swoops out of that gray drizzle, flips into the tumble, and it looks so much like he died that even knowing how it goes I hold my breath until he arcs out and flaps up toward the sky to do it all over again.

I carry the portable back home, letting Old Tumbler come back on his own if he feels like it. The wet is gone, leaving the air hotter and stickier than before. My rebuilt bike leans against the coop next to the Stingray. I run the polishing rag over the sweet curves of those high goosenecks. That warm chrome and waxy smell can almost make a guy forget.

Amazing Grace coos. I look in and see she's sitting in the nesting box with her feathers all fluffed and I know she's got another egg. If I could keep Peabody away, maybe I could still make some bucks. But as soon as I think it, I see that cycle all over again—the hatching, the uglies, the growing, the flapping, the jumping.

The killing.

There's only one thing I can do. Get rid of Peabody. Take him out in a field somewhere and leave him where he can't come home.

Charley watches as I kneel down and pull Peabody into my lap. I scratch the cat behind the ears and feel him purr. Then I stuff him in the portable. There's something just right about that cat going out the same way the birds came in. I balance the portable between the high gooseneck handlebars. It's kind of sad that the bike's first ride is something messed up like this. I wanted to keep it pure.

Charley must have figured out by now what I'm doing, but he just watches. I push off real easy, letting it coast down the trailer park drive, listening to the hum, gliding under the CANTE BURY sign, turning onto the street, and for the first time pressing my feet against the pedals.

Peabody howls 'cause he knows right away the score. There's no noise like a cat howling from fear. I'm thinking of this old movie *Zombie Cats from Outer Space* and I'm seeing Peabody creeping his way back to our trailer, sneaking onto the porch in the middle of the night, creeping up to my couch, and chewing my neck.

I reach the top of the Banzai Run and stop the bike by dragging my feet. The one thing that bike don't got is good brakes. I check out the view clear across the fields and even to the brown hills way across the valley. My Buying Time plan is dead broke. I got only two choices left. Either steal something for real from the old man, or tell the Blackjacks where they can shove it. Only there's no way I can do either one. What choices did they give Cesar Aguilar?

My eyes do the Banzai Run, seven blocks straight downhill. There are three stop signs and two streetlights. It's not so bad now, on a lazy afternoon. But at seven in the a-and-m, the official time, when the commuters are hurrying and the farm machinery is rumbling, Banzai-ing down that hill, running the stop signs, and praying for green lights . . . well, the Banzai is suicide.

Suicide.

I push off down the Run, just taking my sweet time.

Peabody has stopped howling, and the quiet is even creepier than the howl.

I'm doing slow, easy turns back and forth.

I guess I been trying to avoid it for a long time, but as I do the turns, it comes to me and there's no taking it back. I got to make a deal with the Blackjacks. One all-or-nothing scheme. One awesome, final Banzai Run to wipe out all of Buying Time. There's no other way.

This bike is big and clunky compared to the Stingray. But for a straight downhill run, the momentum of the big will work better than the nimble of the small. Getting down as fast as possible is my best chance. Even the Stingray won't get me past a truck lumbering through one of the cross streets. Sure, it would be easier to lay it down on the asphalt, if it comes to that. But if it does come to that, it means the Run is lost. And if the Run is lost, then nothing else matters.

The quiet is still coming at me from that portable as I reach the bottom and cruise onto Mr. Anderson's tomato field. I lift the portable off the handlebars. Peabody is an amateur next to some of the things stalking around here at night. If I let him go, it's as good as killing him. I walk along one of the furrows. Even if I get rid of this cat, Amy will just get another fuzz-ball kitten. And that one will grow up into another killer before you know it. I drop the portable but don't unlatch the door. And then the whole cycle will start all over again. Nothing a guy can do about something like that.

I'm beat.

I lift the portable, lug Peabody back to the bike, and head home.

Charley is still standing by the coop as I glide to a stop and drop the portable on the dirt. I kneel and unlatch the door, but

Peabody stays crouched inside, like he thinks this is another trick. Finally, he bolts out and skitters under the trailer. I stand and squint at Charley, daring him to say something. Of course, he don't. Why am I so pissed off at Charley? None of this is his fault. He's just the watcher.

I stomp across the dirt, grab the Stingray, and put it in front of Charley.

"Take it." He don't move. I grab his hands and force him to hold it. "Take it, damn it."

I step back and take deep breaths.

"Yeah, Charley, it's the perfect size for you." My breathing slows back to normal. "And with that long seat, you can move your foot any way you need it. Get on."

He swings the big foot over the seat and settles in.

"You been practicing when I'm not here, haven't you?"

He grins and stares ahead to wherever he dreams of riding.

"The chain will slip off when you least expect it. I been meaning to fix it, but never got around to it. You're gonna have to do that. Anyway, fixing it will make the bike feel more like it's yours."

He's still staring ahead and not listening to me. I turn away, and I hear the bike crunching the gravel and then bumping onto the asphalt road before I'm even on the porch. I'm going to miss riding that bike. But more than that, I'm going to miss the places it took me.

CHAPTER TWENTY-NINE

FRESH BLOOD

I'm cruising up to Leguin's on the reborn bike I call the Banzai Flyer. The blood-crusty pack is flapping against my back.

I step inside. He sits just like that first time in his suit with the cane across his lap, the bottle of sherry on the table, his melting blue eyes waiting for me.

"I brought you food."

"I have no stomach for food these days." There's a stronger smell to the old man now.

"This is something special."

"Indeed."

I walk into the kitchen and put on a pot of water and light the old stove. It's funny how sounds have this slick way of coming at you. Like the sound of the bottle of Gerber Junior Chicken and Noodles with Peas clicking against the bottom of the pan of boiling water. That flavor was surefire for the sibs when they were finicky toddlers. Then there's the sound of the old man's breathing in the other room, sort of a clucking down in his throat like some kind of pinball on a machine gone tilt. As long as the old man clucks steady like that, I know he's still in his chair and I'm safe for what I finally got the nerve to do. If I'm to make one all-out final deal with the Blackjacks, to pull it off I got to deliver something very real, very primo. Which is why I'm now listening to the mellow thunk of the silverware I'm sliding into my backpack. This is the real thing, heavy pieces wrapped in little velvet bags.

I fix a fancy tray for the old man, figuring that way maybe he won't notice that it's baby food, with a crystal vase with a wildflower I plucked from the yard and a cloth napkin and a for real silver spoon. The Ace won't miss one spoon.

I carry the tray slowly so that the silverware won't rattle in the backpack slung over my shoulder, and set the tray across the arms of the chair, making it into a wannabe high chair. He just sits there staring at the Gerber Junior Chicken and Noodles with Peas, the steam making his cheeks all wet.

"Here," I say, "let me put this other napkin around your neck."

"As though it were a bib."

"Just let me tie—"

"Young man, do not come near me with that."

"But just look at your suit there. You got dried-up food hanging there like snot." I can't look at his eyes. "Sorry, but it's true."

"Yes. Indeed."

I tie it around his neck. But he makes no move at the food.

"Here, let me help." I start to pick up the spoon.

"Unhand that utensil."

"Okay, I was just trying to help."

"Then pour me some sherry."

"Right."

"Now sit," he says.

I ease the backpack down beside my chair, but two knives clunk together. I glance to see if he heard, but he's slurping the Gerber Chicken and Noodles with Peas.

"Something is disturbing you," he says between slurps.

Does he know about the silverware? Should I tell him about Roxanne? But why should I bother to share it with him? What does he care? He'll have to settle for the news about the tumbler.

"My sister's cat killed the baby bird. Didn't even eat it. Just killed for the hell of it."

"Ah. An old story."

"Not to me."

He stops slurping and stares at me. "Indeed."

It's weird how Mr. Leguin has fallen apart this last month. Like he's been holding on, waiting for something, and now his waiting is over and he's just let go.

"Take away the tray. I am finished."

I take the tray and put it on a side table.

"Now tell me why you have stolen my silver and hidden it in that bloody backpack."

I fall back in the chair as an icy wave runs through me. Not fear. What could he do, anyway? He couldn't stop me. He don't even have a phone to call the sheriff. And what could he prove? I don't even think it's guilt I'm feeling. Then what?

I open the backpack so he can see the loot. But I don't take the silverware out.

He is silent.

I could tell him all about the Blackjacks and give reasons and excuses, but it wouldn't mean a thing.

"Take it," he says. "I bequeath it to you. Just get out."

"When you first came here," I say, "I imagined you might be a vampire looking for fresh blood. Maybe I wasn't so far off."

"Maybe you were not."

I stand and shoulder the pack, but don't make a move for the door. This is the end, but it's not how it should be.

"Get out."

"Not yet."

"What?"

"You've tricked me into coming and telling you stories that I haven't told no one." I sit, dropping the backpack close beside me. "So now I'm going to make you listen to one last story, whether you want to hear it or not. And I don't want no interruptions. Then it's over. It's about stealing."

The Tale of Shellfish Boogers and the Baby Jesus

It was Christmas. I was eleven. I was standing in the Great Western Emporium down in San Luis when my mom was shopping. Standing in a store that back then was called the Orient Express. Standing in a corner of the Orient Express called Pearls from the Sea. Staring at this string of pearls just lying on a velvet tray on top of the counter. The saleslady had gone to answer the phone. I shouldn't have even been in that store. I couldn't afford one pearl from that thing. But there had been these great pictures at the entrance that showed these Japanese ladies diving for pearls. When I saw this one picture of a diver's leg caught in this giant clamshell, I had to go in and check it out. I stood there staring and thinking about the two main presents I bought at Christmas. The first was for Baby Jesus, but He wouldn't have no use for pearls. The second was for my mom, and they for sure would look awesome on her.

A sign showed how the pearls were made by the oyster to protect it from grains of sand. I got to thinking that these fancy pearls weren't no more than shellfish boogers. Well, I'd just about convinced myself that I didn't want my mom wearing shellfish boogers around her neck when that necklace was sitting right in my pocket. I mean, my hand just reached out and snatched it without my okay. I took the necklace home and hid it under my mattress on the back porch.

Wouldn't you know it, that same week the teacher brought this huge bucket of little shells to class. We strung fishing line through the shells to make necklaces, and we painted our names to make them personal. When I got back to our trailer after school, I went straight to my mattress and took out the pearl necklace. I hid under the covers and just stared at the two necklaces. One I'd give to my mom and one I'd give to Baby Jesus. But which was which?

I know all about how my mom would like the one that I made because of the sentimental value, like they say. But a guy's experience also tells him that in a couple years that shell necklace will be at the bottom of some drawer along with a clay handprint and a funky ashtray. But a pearl necklace, that wouldn't end up at the bottom of no drawer. She'd wear that every time she went out on a fancy date with a prospect and she'd remember I gave it to her 'cause no prospect ever gave her nothing that awesome, except maybe a baby. But then, if I gave her the pearl necklace, she'd want to know where I got it.

And then there was Baby Jesus to think about, too. Baby Jesus wouldn't appreciate nothing that'd been stolen, that's for sure. Then it came to me, a vision like a saint might get. If Jesus knew everything, why not leave it up to Him to do the right thing? Well, I found two little boxes exactly the same and put one necklace in each box and I wrapped them with the same paper and ribbon and all that so that even I couldn't tell. And if I didn't know which I was giving to my mom and which I was giving to Baby Jesus, then the blame was out of my hands. Jesus would do the choosing.

So that night I sat at the children's Christmas Eve Mass, one hand in each jacket pocket, fingering the small boxes wrapped in shiny gold paper with the mysteries inside. That grammar school chapel, with its white stucco and fake stained glass and squeaky portable pews, is about as different from the mission as . . . well, as all other girls are different from Manny's sister Theresa. There's a feel inside me when

I'm near Theresa that's stronger than around other girls. San Miguel is different from other chapels in sort of the same way. I guess that's some kind of sin, comparing chapels to girls. But if you smelled the mission's cool adobe walls and you felt that all-seeing eye of God with its 3-D rays of light shining over you and you knelt at those smooth oak pews, then you'd know how empty I felt sitting with the sibs at Christmas Eve in those squeaky pews under the fluorescent lights clutching the presents.

The big show at the children's Mass was a lame procession to the manger scene in front of the altar. A high school guy dressed in a dorky bathrobe led the way as Joseph. The wannabe Madonna followed with the Baby Jesus hidden in her robe. When they reached the altar, she took out the wooden Baby Jesus and put it in the manger. Then three more guys from the high school, dressed in bathrobes and crowns, walked up the aisle. They were the three wise guys, as Charley called them. As they passed each row, the kids pushed and shoved their way out of the pews, holding little presents in their hands, and followed the three wise guys.

I led my brothers and sisters out of our pew. I was getting a little old for this, but no one noticed 'cause I hadn't gotten taller. We reached the manger and everyone stood around staring at the Baby Jesus in the for real hay. It wasn't too late for me to back out. Then a little girl stepped up and laid a present in the manger and kissed the Baby Jesus. That broke the mood and there was like a pushing, squirming mess of kids trying to get at that manger.

Soon the other kids wandered back to their seats. But I stood, my hands stuffed in my pockets, eyeballing Baby Jesus. Which box? The wannabe Madonna had this scared look on her face like she thought I was about to do something weird. Then my right hand twitched. Okay, it wasn't much of a sign. But it was all I had. I lifted the present out of my right pocket. The ribbon was messed up, so I straightened it. I held out my offering. The paper was stained with sweat, but that couldn't be helped. I lay the present in His arms and stared at Baby Jesus's face, like He'd nod at my choice or something. But He just stared back with a blank doll's grin.

I turned and walked back, ignoring the stares, and plopped into our pew as the children's choir slid into "Silent Night." My mom's glare cut through me. I felt the song sliding up me like sickening sweet incense, but I gagged it back down. You see, I had sung in the choir for years, but a few months before that Christmas I quit, after she praised my confirmation solo. She'd said I had my dad's same sweet voice.

Well, Christmas Eve was the one time when my mom made all the sibs stay with their fathers' families. They didn't always stay with the fathers, but my mom always dug up some member of the prospect's family. I didn't have any other family, so she was stuck with me.

Christmas mornings I woke before my mom. Every year there'd be a couple things in my stocking and maybe one wrapped present. But the main gift was always the same. I'd wake to see the Lionel train on the figure-eight track that took up the whole floor in front of the tree. My dad had died right after my third Christmas, but he had already bought the old train on layaway at Mrs. Elliot's, and she had delivered it just like he'd ordered.

All the years of that train run in me like trips around that figure-eight track. The hum of the transformer as the red light flickers on. The electric tingle as my tongue licks the track.

The rising hum as I turn the lever and the train edges forward, clicking faster, faster, gliding along the track: first the black engine with its pipes and stacks and the smell of fresh oil and metal, its wheels spun by the metal rods . . . then the fat black coal car, LIONEL on the side . . . then the orange boxcar that said BABY RUTH CANDY but in my head carried teddy bears and wild tigers and friendly hobos and a runaway boy . . . then the flatcar, where I put real stuff like a special rock or a toy car or my mom's shiny present . . . then the red caboose with the little second story where a kid could just kick back, watching the whole scary world glide by without it ever hurting him.

At some point I always stopped the train and pressed the REVERSE button, the train edging slowly back. Then faster, flying backward around the figure eight. Faster and faster . . . But you can't ever take things back to before because that lame train always spun clear off the tracks. Then I put the edges of each wheel of each car back on the track, hooked the cars together, replaced my mom's shiny present back on the flatcar, and started the train forward again.

As I sat and watched my mom's present glide round and round, I never heard her come into the room. Finally, I stopped the train and gave her the present. She unwrapped the shell necklace and put it around her neck, but it slid under all those shiny beads and disappeared.

Nothing was ever said about where that train first came from. Every January sixth, the Epiphany, the train would be stored away someplace where I'd forget about it until the next Christmas. But that Christmas was the last time I saw the train. Now it stays forever stored somewhere inside both our heads.

"Goodbye, Mr. Leguin."

CHAPTER THIRTY

ABSOLUTION

I'm sitting in the beach chair on Mr. Sanders's slab, the blue light bathing me. It's the deepest black of night, but too many questions swirl around in me to sleep. My Rod Carew bat lies across the arms of the chair, and I run my hands on the wood just for comfort.

Waiting. Biding my time. Looking out under CANTE BURY to where we'd played maybe our last over-the-line, only a couple weeks ago. Theresa had come out, the first girl to ever play. And they even picked her over one of the guys. The guy was me. Not one of my best hours. Glad for her, but damn . . . She never went back and played again. When I asked why, she said, "All boys are creeps." Since I'd had to sit on the curb the whole game, I wasn't sure whether she included me as a creep, but she probably did since I'm a boy.

A light flicks on in a nearby trailer. It's the single-wide Buns shares with his mom. His shadow darkens the curtains. He hasn't been home for weeks, staying up with the Blackjacks in the hills. Well, now he's returned, and I got a hunch why. So I sit here waiting. The hard wood of that bat takes on a whole new comfort.

My mind goes back to that night in the old Miller place, and I see Buns's face going purple after I told him he's got bigger tits than Roxanne . . . and then I'm remembering the road to the Corpus Christi, when Buns had said, *You're a part of our initiation*. He had said "a part," and I had let that slide. But now it hits me. The other so-called part must have been Roxanne. I had been half of the initiation, and Roxanne had been the other half. I almost admire the Ace for such a perfect, twisted plan. So Buns has been the connection between Roxanne and the Blackjacks all along. I stand up and step off the slab.

I don't need any light to walk along the gravel path to his trailer. Mr. Sanders's voice whispers behind me, *Violence is not the answer*. I try and block it out as I take some warm-up swings. *Violence is not the answer*.

Buns steps out of the trailer carrying a large duffel bag. He sees me coming and he sees the bat, but he just shrugs and opens the door of the sweet El Camino his father gave him after the divorce. He tosses the duffel on the seat and slides in after it. I know the truck is a metallic blue, but in the darkness it looks black. He slams the door. I stand with the bat over my shoulder, staring at him through the window. He rolls it down like he's afraid I'll smash it.

"Going somewhere?"

"RJ, just let it go."

"Let it go?" I lift the bat.

"Listen. She wanted to go up there."

I swing the bat hard against the front fender, a sting jolting my arms. But it just makes a soft thunk and a small dent.

"RJ, some girls get a kick out of danger, you know?"

I lift the bat and swing again, the sting shooting higher and deeper into me. Still, he just stares back.

"I let her out of purgatory," he says.

"You let her out? You mean she got away?"

He stares straight ahead like at a road only he can see.

"Well, did she get away?"

Silence.

"Tell me, or I go for the headlights. Then you won't be seeing anything."

"You don't get it, RJ. I don't know."

"Don't give me that crap. How could you not know?"

"She just stayed there under that tree. Arms out. Doing that sort of dance of hers."

"Dance?"

"Yeah, like when we were at the Miller place. I tried to snap her out of it. Took her arm. Shook her. Pulled her away. Shit, I was afraid her singing would wake the others. But she wouldn't go. Hell, maybe she was already gone in her mind. Maybe. I guess I could have picked her up or something, carried her. She ain't that big. Finally, she was quiet. But she still wouldn't go. If the Ace found out it was me . . . Jesus. So I left her there."

"Then what?"

"Then in the morning, she was gone."

"So she got away."

"Some of the Jokers, they were acting really creepy. I mean, they'd been crazy for a long time. But this was weird . . . kind of paranoid, you know? And the Ace, he was like in this skull-grinning good mood. Not even caring to find out who let her out. Do you think if she had escaped, he'd be like that? The hell we'd pay. I think she did something to herself up there. Maybe hanged herself. And that one of the older guys, maybe the Ace, found her. And they buried her somewhere."

"But you *think*. You don't know for sure."

"There were whispered stories, mostly among the younger guys. At first, the stories were about what I just said. She hung herself from that tree. Maybe even the ghost of Coyote Jack made her do it. And that the Jokers, they found her and took her off and buried her. And that if any of us tell, we'll end up with her. That her ghost was with Coyote Jack and that ours will be there, too. That's when some of the younger ones really stopped coming."

"The Ace could have made up that rumor," I say. "Because if the others knew she'd gotten away, then he'd lose a lot of his power."

"You think too much, RJ. Anyway, then the tale began to change. Some younger kid was supposed to have been watching that night. No one knows who it was, though. And he was supposed to have seen her with a guy under the tree. And then the guy left her. And she did some weird shit. Then she wandered down the hill like some ghost. And she got away."

"That could have been you, the guy under the tree. And the weird shit is her dancing."

"Could've been. I was scared shitless, afraid that some kid was going to finger me. But that never happened, so I'm thinking it might have just been a story."

"But you don't know for real."

"No. I don't. But . . . I mean, come on, RJ."

"Buns, you gotta go to the sheriff."

"What good would that do?"

I lift the bat, fighting a coldness that might numb the anger.

"Think about it, RJ. They will never find her body. If there is a body. They will never get the proof. And no one will ever testify. She'll always be just a runaway."

He's right. God, I know he's right. Then I see something in his eyes. He feels like he *deserves* to have his truck smashed. He's almost welcoming it. Each smash would be like the click of a bead in a twisted rosary. The last thing I want is for him to feel absolution.

I drop the bat.

He turns on the ignition and the pipes growl.

His mother stares at us through the curtained light, like some ghost spying on us from a safer world.

"Where are you going?"

"LA to live with my dad." He glances at the trailer window.

"What about MJB?"

"He already got away. His dad sent him to some private school in Carmel."

"And Ed the Head?"

"He didn't make it. He thinks he's found a way to escape, strung out all the time."

The truck rumbles toward the gate and I follow until he drives under the sign and turns onto the street. I head back to my chair.

I got one last tale to tell.

Even if there is no one to hear it.

The Tale of Foxy Roxy and a Bad Place

There was a girl. War killed her father when she was little. She had no sibs to share her loneliness. Just a mom who treated her bad. And her mom's boyfriends, who treated her even worse. She had half a brother, but she was jealous of him, and so she was mean to him. She thought that was how you treated someone you loved. The boy didn't know no better, either, so he treated her the same way back.

A lot of bad things were done to her. So many that they became a part of who she was, and so she started doing the bad stuff to herself because she didn't know another way.

She tried to get better. She even went to God thinking He would help. But she didn't find anything there. She thought that was her last chance. So if God wouldn't help, she would go to the opposite. She went to a very, very bad place. And very bad things happened to her. Those things nearly killed her.

A boy helped her out of this purgatory. But it wasn't over. There was still evil pulling at her. Whispers that she belonged there. That she was so bad, she couldn't ever be good. It was a terrible battle between her and that bad thing.

But she won that battle.

In the wee hours before dawn, she turned away from that evil and made her way down the gorge. She sneaked back home and got her clothes and stuff and packed them in a bag. Then she sneaked out and found a truck driver who drove her down to Santa Maria.

Once she was out of that valley, she began to feel cleaner. That evil was back there, no longer inside her.

She got a job as a waitress. She didn't do no more bad stuff. Well, she did some. But nothing as bad as before. And the more she stayed there, the less bad stuff she did.

She met a good guy. He was a little older. But he had a good job. A schoolteacher, maybe. They got married. They had a kid. She named him Richard. Ricky for short. They lived as happily ever after as most people.

And this is the for real truth.

CHAPTER THIRTY-ONE
SUICIDE CITY

I wake up with Charley shaking my shoulder. Daylight streams through the screens. He drags me outside as I pull on my jeans.

Amazing Grace lies on the dirt. Her neck is all chewed up. The Old Tumbler sits on the roof of the coop, cooing.

Peabody done this.

There's only one thing left to do.

I wrap Amazing Grace in the rag I use to polish the Banzai Flyer and load the Old Tumbler in the portable. I head for Mr. Anderson's tomato field by way of Eighth Street instead of the Banzai. There's only one Banzai Run left in me, and I got to save that.

I bury her in the middle of the field, deep enough so she won't get dug up. Then I let the Old Tumbler go. He heads straight for the sky, but I turn away without watching his fall through that heat. I leave the portable lying in the field and start for home. The Old Tumbler won't have trouble finding his way. But a part of me hopes he takes off to find a better place.

I get home, slip into the trailer, and pull the backpack out from under the sofa bed, the silverware thunking as I lift it onto my back. It's time to make my final delivery to the Blackjacks.

And so I make my way up Dead Man's Gorge. There are no Deuces. What's left of the campsite is a mess.

The Ace is sitting under his tree like I remembered, one leg of those old jeans over the arm of the rattan chair with his cracked boot just dangling and his elbow on the other arm, with his chin resting on his fist and his face a shadow under that Raiders cap. I stare at the black limb above his head and think of Roxanne. I can't let the hate and sad fill me now or I won't ever get through this.

"You're late," he says.

"What do you mean, late?"

He nods and two guys stand right behind me. "I was expecting you days ago."

I pull the pack off my back without answering. The silver makes rich, mellow clunks.

The Deuces are gone, run away back to their homes. Like Buns said. Now only some of the older guys are left. This makes them even more dangerous.

"My delivery from the old man." I work to keep my voice flat.

"Let me see what you got." The Ace takes off his cap and wipes the sweat from his stubs.

I kneel and spread out the silver.

"Bring me one."

The gray-haired guy picks up one of the knives and brings it to him.

The Ace hefts it. "This is good stuff. The real deal."

He waves to his two sidekicks to take Mr. Leguin's silver away.

"Why did you risk bringing it up here, RJ?"

"I got a proposal for you. A deal."

"Now, why would we want to make any deals? What do you got that we couldn't just take?"

"Me."

"You? We already got you."

"Me and the Banzai Run."

"Go on."

"I do the Banzai Run. If I make it, you leave me . . . and the old man . . . alone."

"It don't make sense. What do I get by you running the Banzai that would be worth losing what I'm already getting from the old man?"

"Well . . . it will . . . make you famous."

"Famous?"

"Yeah. Everyone remembers the last run of Cesar Aguilar. It's a legend."

"Yeah, I remember that run myself. It was my first year as a Blackjack." He looks around, and I can see he's thinking this might be a way to get back some of the mojo. Then he frowns. "It got more fame for Cesar than for the Blackjacks. You got to do better than that, RJ."

"Well, for another thing, you can make some big bucks off this."

"How?"

"Make bets."

"You gotta be kidding. It takes two sides to make a bet. Who would be stupid enough, even with odds, to bet you'd make it? The only way we could make money off a bet like that would be for *us* to bet you *will* make it. We'd get a whole lot of takers against that bet. Then we'd fix it so you really would make it. Yeah, we'd clean up on that. But that would spoil all the fun and miss the main point."

"Okay, then, you could charge."

"Charge?"

"Yeah, charge a fee for watching."

"On public streets? Why, this is a free country." He laughs like that's the best joke he's ever made.

"And how long have you been charging kids for 'protecting' them on public streets?"

He stops laughing. Now he's thinking about it.

"Besides," I say, keeping it rolling so he can't think on it too long, "guys will *want* to pay."

"Why's that?"

"Paying makes them a part of it. If they want to be a part of it—and who won't want to be a part of someone dying on the Banzai Run—they gotta pay. You can even say I won't do it unless you raise so much money. Like one of those events where guys run so many miles for charity."

"I like that . . . a benefit fundraiser for the Blackjacks. You know, if you weren't such a loser, you could have been sitting here one day." His hand reaches out, and his fingers curl for me to move closer. He leans forward like it's just the two of us. "I know what you're thinking," he says in a singsong voice. "You're thinking you might be able to survive that Run. In fact, maybe . . . just maybe you got an angle. Some angle I haven't thought about yet. Yeah, that would be just like you."

"Yeah. I got an angle. And I'll tell you."

"Well?"

"The angle is that I don't care if I make it or not."

"Go on."

"I'm free either way. If I make it, I'm free. If I don't make it, then I'm free in a different way."

"Welcome to Suicide City. It runs through your family."

His words gut-punch me.

He spreads his lips and shows his teeth like he's supposed to be smiling. "I'm beginning to like this idea." Then his mouth tightens and his voice goes so low I lean closer to hear. "If I think you're holding back on that Run, if I so much as suspect you're not going all out, the deal is off. Then you'll be begging to die quick."

"There's only one way to do the Banzai." I breathe slow and deep. "Balls out."

"Then it's set. You'll do it Friday. Seven thirty a.m. And no helmet, or any of that other new BMX armor crap."

"Can't afford it, even if I cared."

"And if you chicken out, or you try and pull a fast one, then think about your brother."

"Charley? What's that supposed to mean? He's got nothing to do with this."

"He does now."

"He's only a pain in the ass, anyway."

"Nice try. You screw us over, do any double crosses, and it won't just be you that suffers."

"Then there's two sides to that deal. If I *do* make the run, no matter how it turns out, you leave Charley alone."

The wicker chair groans as he makes a half shrug, half nod. I turn to leave.

"Oh, I nearly forgot to tell you," he says.

I turn back, still feeling the ache in my gut.

"We know about your little scheme."

"What scheme?"

"Where you been getting the loot."

"What are you talking about?"

"I'm talking about how you've been buying stuff instead of stealing it from the old man. We've had a great time watching you. Nice of you to spend all your money at that old witch's Emporium, and still leave all the old man's stuff for us to take when we want."

I turn to leave again. There's nothing else to say.

"No matter what happens, RJ," he calls, "the old man is ours. This deal don't got nothing to do with him."

CHAPTER THIRTY-TWO

NEON BLUES

I'm kneeling on the hardpack dirt in front of Charley, who's stretched out in a beach chair in the shade of the Silverstream as I wash his messed-up foot one last time. Mom has taken the other sibs for the afternoon, and I want to finish with Charley before they get home. The odor of Epsom salt, baking soda, and rosemary swirling in warm water wafts out of the old pickle bucket next to me.

I massage deep into the muscles, feeling how the foot has now stretched longer than a child's and spread wider than mine. Only one toenail is left, and it's not clear which toe it nails. At least there aren't sores and blisters no more. Instead, the heel and arch have hardened into deep callouses that'll keep him from hurting.

"I don't know about you, Charley, but I'm thinking our toe show days are long gone." I knead my thumbs into the ball of the foot, digging for pain, but he only returns that smile. "You still think there's some Greater Purpose to it all?"

He nods.

"Damn you." I might feel like one of those shoe salesladies, but there's no way I'm dripping any tears on that sorry appendage. No freaking way. I dry the pink skin with an old cloth and then slide the Chuck back on. He don't wear socks. Then I stand, lug the bucket over to the weeds, toss out that gunky mess, and return to Charley. He's still sitting there like some garden cherub.

"You think you're some kind of prince just 'cause I massaged your feet again? Lace up and follow me. I ain't done with you yet."

I lead our sorry two-kid pilgrimage to the unlit CANTE BURY.

"You might have to take over the sign, so pay attention."

Charley stands facing me beneath the tubes.

"This time of day is called the blue hour. You know, when it's not day no more, but it's not night, either? That's the best time to do the sign."

Even though other guys are freaked by his stare, I'll honestly miss it. I lug the rickety aluminum ladder under the sign and unfold it. Then I pull the old sock out of my back pocket.

"Take this. No, it ain't for your foot. You're going to need to clean the sign once in a while. But you shouldn't use soap and water, or any of that spray stuff. You got that? So what I do is, I wear the sock like a glove. That way I can feel the curve of the tube through my hand. Then I run the sock over the tubes to wipe off the dirt."

Charley nods and pulls the sock over his perfect little hand.

"Okay, here's the tricky part." I hold the bottom of the ladder. "You're gonna climb up."

He grabs the metal and lifts his good foot onto the first

rung, then pulls the big foot after it. The ladder shifts. I hold it still. He climbs the second step and it wobbles and I clutch it tighter. A third step and more wobbling and I brace my feet. I look up. He's high enough to reach the C, but he's going to need another step to touch the rest of the word. I wrap my arms around the ladder.

"Okay. One more."

The wobbling stops. He's drifted into his safe place, and the ladder's gone perfectly still. I don't have to hold it now, but I do just in case. He runs his socked hand gently along the C and up the A, and then steps to the top rung to reach the highest curve.

"That's enough. Come on down now."

He descends as easily as some wannabe angel out of the sky, and then I wrestle the ladder to the other side and we do it all over. When he's back on solid ground again, I hug him.

"Good job. Look at me." I make sure he zeroes in on my eyeballs. "You never do this alone. You have the twins, or Amy if you can get her to do it, spot the ladder for you. Now you take the ladder and collapse it."

He wrestles it down, but I don't help him.

"Okay, now slide the ladder under the ivy there against the fence. Even if someone sees it there, they won't bother to steal that clunky thing."

Then I kneel below the sign and find the heavy plug in the weeds.

"It's grounded, so it's pretty safe. Still, don't try this if it's raining, or even foggy. The socket is down here against the supporting post." I look up to see if he's paying attention, and he nods. "It's the argon that gives the tubes their blue. But the gas ain't getting to that middle section no more. Nothing we can do about that now."

I plug it in, and CANTE BURY buzzes and then hums. I stand. Charley and me are bathed in that blue light.

"I'm going to need you tomorrow, Charley."

"Okay."

"It's for the Banzai Run."

"I know."

"Tomorrow, you're going to be my squire, like back in King Arthur days. A knight always had a squire to stand by him and hand him his shield or whatever, and then he'd watch him win the joust or kill the dragon, that kind of thing. You'll do that. Be my squire."

"What about Manny?" he asks.

"What about him?"

"Won't he be there?"

"No."

"Why?"

"He don't want to be a part of it."

I wait for the next why, but he just nods.

"I might get hurt tomorrow. You understand?"

He nods again.

"I mean real bad hurt."

Charley's body goes still and he begins to drift into that invisible place.

"Stop it." I grab his shoulders and stare into his eyes. "I see you, Charley. I *see* you."

"You're hurting me," he says.

"Well, you save your superpower thing in case you run across Blackjacks. Don't waste it on me." My fingernails are dug into his shoulder, and I pull back.

"Okay."

"One last thing. The old man at the Miller place. He's close to dying, but—"

"I'm sorry, RJ."

"Huh? What are you talking about?"

"I should have been a better lookout. I shouldn't have fallen asleep."

"Have you been thinking it was your fault this whole time?"

He nods.

"Oh, Charley."

CHAPTER THIRTY-THREE
BANZAI

I straddle the great Banzai Flyer at the top of the Run.

"This is stupid." Charley is sitting on the curb next to the Stingray that's now his, staring and muttering.

Even at seven thirty a.m. it's hot and sticky. There's a low, sad fog that'll burn off sometime on the other side of this. I smell my own scared sweat and the bike's wax and oil and the asphalt underneath.

"This is the stupidest."

"You're not sounding like a squire, Charley. You got to be strong."

Guys stand in clusters down the run. The Banzai Flyer deserves better. I guess I pictured something heroic with the sun shining off the Flyer and crowds of people cheering and screaming and then I soar down the Run like a flipped-out tumbler. Whatever happens, it won't be that.

Damn you, Manny. I thought for sure he'd be here last-minute.

My eyes make one last pretend run: Down that first steep block that gives you the speed and on into the first intersection. No problem. There's a stop sign going the other way, so as soon as a car brakes, the driver will look up and see you Banzai-ing down the run and have a spaz attack and let you fly on by. Down the second block with a second stop sign. A heavy-duty bump to handle right in the middle of the road. Down the third block to the first traffic light. An official lookout is waiting there. He'll eyeball the street going the other way and lift his arms up in the all-clear sign. Down two more blocks and another light. Another official lookout. Down the last block, where the Banzai Run dumps onto Murietta Street at a T intersection. As you cross that intersection, you angle for that crazy driveway that takes you onto Mr. Anderson's tomato field.

I twist the taped-up handlebars, waiting for both lookouts to have their arms raised at the same time. That'll be the signal to go for it. The theory is that if you're fast enough and lucky enough, you can make it through both lights. Of course, since no one has really made it, it's only a theory. The two official lookouts are Jokers.

Then I see Theresa sitting on the roof of a house halfway down the Run, where she has a clear view all the way to the end. Her knees are up under her chin, her arms wrapped around her legs. Her ponytail is undone and her hair hangs around her shoulders like a shawl.

What sucks—really sucks—is that seeing her makes me care whether I'll make it.

The Ace stands at the bottom of the Run.

The first lookout has his arms raised.

There's one small problem with the Great Banzai Flyer.

The brakes. It's got pedal brakes, but if you lean back with all your weight, the best you can hope for is a big hum and a little slow. There's no point even thinking about brakes now. I'm going to the bottom all-out. No brakes. No slowing. No matter what.

The second lookout is raising his arms so that both lookouts got their arms all the way raised at the same time.

"This is ultra stupid." Charley stares at the curb, refusing to look down the Run.

A sound drifts up at me from the small groups of guys lining the street: "Banzai, Ban-ZAI, BAN-ZAI!"

I lean back and push off, my toes giving a last grab at the asphalt.

"BBBAAAANNNNNNNZZZZZIIIII!"

My stomach drops down to my butt as I fly off the end of the world. The wind sucks my scream inside out. I'm in for the ride and nothing can stop it now.

I scrunch up near the handlebars, squinting my eyes against the wind . . . my feet trying to push through the pedals . . . my whole body all-out scared.

"BAN-ZAI!" rips out of the wind as I fly past the first group of guys.

The tape on the handlebars is soaked with sweat. But this isn't how it should be. If I'm going to fly, it's got to be full-bore crazy. I force myself to sit up. Screw all of them! Then something happens. I stop moving. One second my tires are spinning a mile a minute and I'm flying by parked cars and light posts, and then it's like I'm stopped. Just sitting there. And the world is flying by me. Car door handles and hubcaps shoot past going uphill, curb numbers wiggle by like supersonic worms, the asphalt rolls by underneath me, and I'm just sitting there, kicking back, feeling the ground spin.

"BAN-ZAI, BAN-ZAI, BAN-ZAI." The chant drifts past the whistling in my ears like something out of a dream.

The first block is gone and there is no point pedaling 'cause I'm going too fast for it to do any good. I keep my eyes squinted against the wind and focus on the street—a bump or crack could mean a total wipeout.

The first light is red for me, but the lookout has his hands raised in the all-clear sign. It wouldn't make a difference if they weren't. I fly through the intersection, my feet trying to push clear through the pedals. A bump in the road rushes at me, then rises up under the tires. I crouch down and lift off the seat as the bike sails into the air and comes down cleanly, back tire first. Damn, I'm hot.

Some old guy is backing out of his driveway without even bothering to look up the street. Careless drivers are a real pain. He turns his head. We stare into each other's eyes, and that expression on his face makes me almost laugh. He slams to a stop. But his bumper hangs out in the road right smack in front of me. I swerve and clear it with inches to spare. No problem. Until I try and straighten out. The front wheel starts to wobble right up through my gut. The cars parked along the opposite curb are flying at me. But the good old Banzai Flyer rights itself in the nick of time, and I'm zooming downhill again. Any other bike would have eaten it right there.

Now it's just the blur and twist of the road and the wind ripping at me. It's like I'm in this other world where there's no real time, no Blackjacks, no old man, no suicides.

I'm just free-falling.

The tires skid on oil, jerking me back to the for real, and

I straighten out. The second lookout is flying at me, his arms raised in the all-clear sign. He's laughing. He keeps looking at me, then down the street, then back at me. And all the time he's just laughing.

The light is red. I fly into the intersection. I don't really see the car. More like I feel it. Barreling right down on top of me. A black force screaming at me from the right side. The squeal of tires. Smell of rubber. The rush of air at my backside as that car misses me by inches.

"BAAANNNZZZAAAIIII!" I scream. Nothing can get me! I laugh. Nothing!

I'm just free-falling . . .

Free-falling . . .

Freeeee!

The bike tilts forward as it hits the last two, steepest blocks. The Ace's face is buried in the shadow of his baseball cap.

Anderson's driveway is flying up at me just to the left.

I'm past the last house and humming toward the final T intersection.

I'm going to make it!

And there it is, just ahead and to my right, barreling straight at where I'm going to be . . . one of those huge tractor trucks with the high wheels looking like a giant bug, hauling two trailers with slat sides bulging with tomatoes. My only chance is to clear the T and make the driveway before it passes. I fight against legs trying to push back on the brakes.

I see the bugs splattered against the massive truck grille rushing at me.

God, if only I could pull out and fly back up to the sky.

The truck's horn blasts against me.

Screaming-humming-screeeching . . .
A burning smell.
Acid in my throat.
Then I'm flying.
Really flying.
Blackness . . .
. . . I wake up staring up into that empty sky.

People are standing over me. *Jesus, what a mess,* some guy is saying. I know I'm hurt, but I don't feel nothing. Except this wetness on my belly and legs. There's this funny smell. My hand is almost too heavy to lift. I run it across my belly and legs. It touches something wet and sticky. I lift it in front of my eyes. Red.

Then blackness . . .

When I wake up again, I'm still in that field, except I've been moved. A man in a white jacket stares down at me and I'm on this stretcher thing with wheels. That huge tractor truck is halfway onto the field. The trailers are sort of rolled over in the soft ground. Man, there are tomatoes everywhere.

"Am I dying?" I hear myself whisper.

The guy looks at me. "No. But if that driver gets ahold of you, you'll wish you were."

That's no way to talk to a dying kid.

"What about the blood?" I ask.

"Blood?" He laughs. He actually laughs.

He lifts my hand to my mouth, and I taste the tomatoes.

There's blackness like looking through the wrong end of binoculars. The blackness is starting to close in. They roll me into the back of the ambulance. I see the Ace's back framed by the door.

The blackness is closing in.
It's not all over.
The blackness . . .
Not all over . . .

CHAPTER THIRTY-FOUR
CRAZED BALLOONS

Charley steps from the trailer into the porch room holding a breakfast tray. He's been waiting on me like he thinks he can pay me back for all the times I took care of his toes. He sets the tray on the table next to my bed. GET WELL balloons bump against the ceiling above him and I have that same floating feeling, like my head is bobbing around waiting for the rest of me to show up so I'll be heavy enough to stay down. I close my eyes . . .

Hey, kiddo.

"Mom?" I open my eyes and squint against the colors of her beads and yellow muumuu. Charley is gone, and one of the balloons is drooping toward the floor. She looks over at the empty tray. "You feel up to a visitor, maybe two?"

"Suurree . . ." I close my eyes.

RJ?

It's her freckles that first shimmer into the for real. Then her hair brushes my arm and she's sitting on the edge of the bed.

"Theresa?"

"I'm sorry," she says. "I didn't understand about your birds . . . the flying, and all . . ."

I drift away. When I open my eyes again she's still there.

"You know," she is saying as my eyes flicker open, "they picked me for over-the-line just to get back at you. Not 'cause they thought I could play."

My mind drifts, but I keep my eyes open so she won't disappear, until I figure out she's talking about that last over-the-line.

"I should've walked away when I saw you sitting on that curb." I feel her body shift on the bed.

"No, you shouldn't . . . have . . ." I mumble. "The joke is on them."

"What?"

I drift again and wait for my brain to form the words. "You are better than me . . . better . . . than all of them . . ."

RJ. You awake?

A sharp pain smacks the bruise on my shoulder.

I open my eyes and Manny is staring down at me. He's wearing our black tee and jeans, but looking more like Nino every day.

"Damn, Manny, did you just slug me?"

"Yeah, I did."

"Wha . . . why . . ."

"Theresa just kissed you and ran out, dude."

"But I wasn't even awake to . . ."

"Well, we're good now. She was gonna kiss someone someday—she wasn't ever gonna be a nun—so it might as well be you. Just don't do it again."

"But I didn't even do it . . . the first . . . time . . ."

RJ, wake up . . . Doctor says you should stay awake as much as you can.

"Suurree . . . I'm awake."

"Man, you're a freaking legend now."

"Yeah? . . . You should have been there, Manny. You left me hanging, dude."

"Listen to me. I went with Nino-'n-Smitty up Dead Man's Gorge when you were doing the Banzai."

"What . . ."

"Only a couple guys were there. The rest were down watching the Run. They ran off just seeing Nino. Nino-'n-Smitty burnt the tree. Well, they half burnt it. They were worried the hills would catch fire."

"So that's why you weren't there?"

He looks away. "There's only the Ace and a few of the Jokers left. Some of the others got the guts to leave after they saw you do the Run. But you got to watch out. They're full bore, and they're out to get you even more than before. The old man, too."

I try to focus on his words, but they're weaving in and out like a dream.

"Hey, RJ, it's like you're a million miles away. You in pain?"

"Feels like I been beat all over. Doctor says no broken bones . . . I got a concussion." I laugh and then don't know why I'm laughing and so I laugh again.

"What can I do?"

"Tell me a story, something funny."

He's quiet, and I hold back another laugh just watching his eyebrows scrunch as he tries to find himself a story.

"*Bueno,*" he finally says. "Remember that Lone Ranger

set I gave you when we were little? It had a mask and a toy gun and silver bullets. It wasn't your birthday or nothing."

"Yeah, I remember."

"Didn't you ever wonder? I mean, I didn't have money to just go and buy something like that without it being a birthday or nothing."

"No, I didn't wonder. I just figured you stole the stuff and you were fencing it to me so Abuelita wouldn't catch you."

"I didn't steal it," he says.

"Yeah? Is this the story?"

"You tell this story to anyone, RJ, and I'll . . ."

I lift two shaky fingers. "I swear."

"Adelita and Maria were taking me shopping with them over in San Luis. Nino-'n-Smitty had just fixed up that little red Ford Falcon convertible that Adelita and Maria shared. You remember that car? They dressed me in my Sunday jacket, put me in the middle of the back seat, and drove with the top down into San Luis."

I lie back and listen to his voice like through a fuzzy speaker. It's good to have someone else do all the talking.

"They got me a haircut, the shortest I ever had. I kept rubbing my head, feeling the skin under the fuzz. They took me to the store and let me pick any toy under five dollars. Remember, RJ, you were *loco* on that Lone Ranger from those black-and-white Saturday-morning reruns? Galloping around with the *heigh-ho Silver mierda* and *ta-tum-ta-tum*ing that song. So when I saw that set with the toy gun and the silver bullets and the mask, I picked that. Then they took me to JC Penney. We went to the ladies' section. To the ladies' underwear section.

"Hey, RJ. You listening to me?"

"Suuure. Ladies' underwear . . ." I laugh.

"The women were all fussing over me. I got the jacket, I got the cut, and at seven *gordito* can be cute. Adelita sat me down in a chair next to a table piled with *chones*. Maria was behind me, telling the saleslady about our Abuelita, who embarrassed them because she wouldn't go out to buy any new bras. So they were going to buy a bra for her. I was holding that Lone Ranger set on my lap still wrapped in the plastic. Maria told the saleslady they didn't know Abuelita's size but they got that part figured out 'cause they brought something about the same size. Then I felt this silky thing slide over my head, and I knew right away it was a bra cup. All the ladies were giggling. *That one is too small*, Maria says. Adelita ordered me to look up 'cause I'm staring down at that Lone Ranger mask locked in the plastic. *That one is too big*, Maria says. Then I felt this stiff cup fit right over my head and I knew what was coming: *That one is just right!*"

I'm laughing so hard I got to hold my head to keep my brain from popping.

Manny ain't laughing, though, and I try and hold back in case he didn't want it to be funny, but it's no use. "Don't know if that's all made-up, but I didn't know you could lay down a tale like that."

"You're the one who taught me to lie, RJ. But that story is the truth. There's more. When we got home, I gave that Lone Ranger package to you without even opening it 'cause I didn't want it no more."

"Manny, you got to admit there's a funny side."

"I watched you all these years," he says like he don't hear me, "and I always remember you back when you were seven with that Lone Ranger shit. 'Cause that's what you are, RJ, a *pinche* Lone Ranger. It's like you ride from one adventure to another, without ever letting anyone touch you. All these years and no one can get close to you except maybe Charley, and maybe not even him."

"That was a great story, but you shouldn't have messed it up with a moral."

"There's something else. Listen to me, RJ. I ain't playing Tonto ever again."

Don't know what that means . . .

"RJ! I'm done with that, you hear me?"

I'll think on it later . . . All I see are the Blackjacks' faces bobbing . . . bobbing like these crazed balloons.

CHAPTER THIRTY-FIVE
ABLUTIONS

Something is wrong. Something that just woke me. Not a dream, something wrong outside the trailer. A numbness around the edge of my brain that makes it hard to think. It's too quiet outside. Very dark and very quiet. Something . . . someone was just here. I feel it. I sit up on the edge of the bed. The room spins. A balloon skitters on the floor. My head feels like there's a freaking worm nibbling at my brain.

I pull on my jeans and T-shirt and slip on my shoes. I walk to the screen door, the floor making waves under me. It feels like the end of night, the sky fading to purple at the edge. What is it about the color purple? I should remember . . . The first bird screeches somewhere far away. I step out the door, down the back steps, and around the empty coop.

A red pentagram drips from the side of the trailer and in my head I'm back in that farmhouse facing old man Leguin for the first time with Charley asleep on the floor. But this pentagram is in the for real. It covers the toe end of the trailer where the sibs sleep. It's still dripping fresh blood.

Peabody lies in the dirt with a crushed head. I'm moving like in a dreamworld . . . getting rags . . . wrapping the body . . . fighting down the gagging . . . and dry heaving on the hard dirt. I bury Peabody out in the field.

Then I stumble through the back door and step up out of the dreamworld back into the real trailer and I go to the can and scrub my face, my hands, my arms, scrub until it hurts. Then scrub some more. I swallow a couple aspirins and run my head through the water. The pentagram and Peabody aren't just about revenge. The Blackjacks have sent me a warning.

No. An invitation.

I put the bottle of aspirin in my jeans pocket and sneak past a sleeping Charley out to the Stingray. The Banzai Flyer is dead. I promised Charley the Stingray, but he'll have to wait. I hop on and kick off and glide under the dark sign and onto the street. The chain holds—Charley has already fixed it. Then I ride, pedaling like all my trips to Mr. Leguin's have melted into this one.

My right side throbs from the bruises and my legs ache as I pedal. The head pain is creeping back. But the gliding through this cool air has cleared my brain a little. The sky is pink around the edge but still dark blue overhead. Black clouds are drifting up over Big Mama from the ocean. There's a feel and smell in the air that hasn't been there all summer. It's going to rain.

Even from the top of the hill, the old man's house looks wrong. I leave the bike in the bushes at the top of the hill and creep down. The pain is back in my head like the little worms are feeding again. There's a black dot flicking down the sky. So even the Old Tumbler came back to the old man. It's sad seeing that even he couldn't escape all this.

Where are the Blackjacks? I stick to the shadows and come up behind the sheds. There's no sound except my own breathing. The root cellar is off to my left. I edge along the shed until I come to the corner where I see the house. It's a dark shadow against the dawn. The front door hangs open on one hinge. I force my feet to move, one after the other, across the yard to the house. The windows are jagged edges of glass. I sit on the porch step like I'm between two worlds, and I almost reach for a glass of sherry that isn't there, and hear a whistle laugh that's only in my brain. I shake my head and bite my lip until I taste blood to force myself back to the here and now. Then I stand up and walk through the busted door.

The old man's chair and couch have been slashed to shreds. Pieces of a spindly-legged table and broken glass litter the floor. My footsteps echo on bare wood. The sliding door is closed. I open it and blackness oozes out at me.

"It's time you visited the root cellar." Leguin's voice scratches out of that dark like little bird pecks, and it's no dream.

"I thought you were . . . I was afraid you'd be . . ." I'm standing at the doorway, talking at the big shadow in the corner that I know is his bed.

"Dead? They have been afraid to kill me, thus far. This destruction is merely the residue of their fear, a fear that inevitably will lead them here. We have little time remaining."

"Right. We got to get you out of here." At least my headache has faded back to little wormholes.

"First you will take me to the root cellar." Now I can just make out his outline sitting up in bed, propped against the wall.

"No way. I gotta get you off this place before they come back."

"Light it," he says.

The candelabra sits on the dresser. I use a match to light enough candles to give the room some flicker. He's wearing that funky brown suit.

"Okay, let's go."

"Over here." He nods at the floor by his bed.

I take a breath and step closer, knocking something that clinks on the floor—empty jars of Gerber Chicken and Noodles with Peas.

"Water." He nods at a for real gold cup lying in all that mess.

"You want water? There's no time. They could come back any moment. You can have all you want to drink when we're gone. Come on, let me help you out."

"No." Rank breath seeps up out of his mouth.

"We got to—"

"First water. Then the root cellar."

Root cellar? I've got two choices: drag him out kicking and clawing, or go along with his craziness as fast as I can and hope I can coax him out of here before the Black-jacks return.

"Okay, I'll get water from the kitchen. Then we haul ass out of here. We do the root cellar another time."

I grab the gold cup and rush to the kitchen and fill it and rush back.

"Here." I hold it to his lips.

"No." He jerks his head away. "Put it down. Take off my stockings."

Great. Just when I think things can't get no more weird.

"I ain't . . ."

His eyes in that candlelight stop me. The melting blue has frozen into these ice cubes surrounded by the web of wrinkles.

"Ablutions," he says.

"I don't know what you're talking about, but we gotta get out of here."

"We must perform ablutions to purify and humble us."

"I showered yesterday, and I already been humbled plenty."

"First, you will wash my feet." He twists around so his feet are dangling over the side of the bed and his wrinkles all scrunch up around the eyes, showing some kind of major pain.

"Like hell." But there's something that's got hold of me and there's no choice but to follow it to the end. "Okay. Let's get it over with." I hold my breath, kneel down in front of him, and grab a black sock that don't hide the twisted thing inside it. I picture Charley and all our trips to the shoe salesladies.

I pull off the sock and stare down at clawed toes and a foot swollen like he'd walked barefoot across India like some pilgrim.

"Yes, I am afraid they are grotesque. Arthritis. We are in something of a hurry. I suggest you begin."

"Huh? Right . . ."

"Dip your fingers in the bowl, and then lightly wash the feet, proceeding downward, culminating in the toes."

Even though it looks melted, his heel feels dry. Like it'll crinkle up and blow away. I rub the water around on his skin, feeling his stare, but I don't look up. I got to be one sick dude, 'cause this is like the closest I ever felt to another person in my whole life. Even closer than to Charley.

"Now finish by sprinkling a little of this, and I will do your feet." He's holding a glass bottle with a picture of the Virgin etched on the side.

"Is that holy water?"

"It's from Lourdes."

"We could use us a miracle about now." I sprinkle the water over his toes.

"I have been saving this for longer than you can imagine."

Nothing happens. I knew it wouldn't. "Maybe it passed its expiration date."

He whistle-laughs. "Now it is time for your ablutions. You will have to hold the bowl. I'm afraid my hands are not capable of that."

"You ain't touching my feet." Why hadn't I ever thought of being on the other side of this? "No way."

"Indeed, I am." He climbs off the bed and his whole body is shaking from the pain. "It is necessary."

I sit on the edge of the bed and undo the laces. He pulls off my left shoe and sock. A shiver goes up me when his claws touch my bare foot. The water is cool. His hands shake, but they're gentle, like when he was holding the Old Tumbler. His fingers slide along my heel, over the bottom, around the side, down the top, and then touch the toes.

I close my eyes.

Maybe when I open them I'll be back on the porch that first day and this'll all have been just a nightmare. I open my eyes. But I'm not back on the porch that first day. The old man is still hunched up in front of me like one of the shoe salesladies. But that don't mean this isn't a nightmare. He grabs my other foot.

He stops before he gets to the toes. He's breathing hard, trying to hold in the pain. "I . . . I'm afraid that will have to do." He leans against the side of the bed, sucking air.

"I got some aspirin."

He shakes his head.

"Yeah, I guess you need something a whole lot stronger."

"Truly. But I cannot use it. My mind must remain clear."

"What now?"

He nods at the drawer in the nightstand. I open it. There's a pistol inside.

"It is a German Luger," he says.

It's small. Blunt and square around the trigger, soft and curving at the handle. It's real old.

"Take it out."

"Man, it's heavy." It's clean and reeks of oil, but it couldn't have been fired in a million years. "You want to use this old thing against the Blackjacks?"

"You see some papers in the bottom of the drawer?"

"Yeah."

"Those are copies of documents leaving all of this to your mother."

"I don't . . ."

"You will have to carry me. The pain is more than I can endure. You will have to make two trips—one for me, and one for the candelabra, bowl, and gun."

"Okay, okay. Here, I'll carry you piggyback."

"The indignity."

"You got to trust me on this," I say. "I got experience."

"Indeed."

I sit on the edge of the bed. He wraps his claws around my neck. I choke back a gag. I stand, holding his legs that are only sticks and loose skin inside that greasy suit. I haul him to the living room.

"Perhaps I should walk."

"I can do this."

I stagger to the front door and kick the screen open. Dark clouds swirl overhead. I carry him across the yard, cloud shadows creeping on the ground.

The sound is far away, maybe the top of the hill. It's like a half scream, half laugh. It's coming this way. I glance back at the old man, but his face doesn't show that he hears them.

"I suggest a brisk pace," he says.

"Brisk pace, hell. We gotta leave."

"Do not panic."

"Yeah, sure. Don't panic." I lie him next to the root cellar door.

"Now go back to the house. I want you to bring the candelabra, the bowl, and the gun. Hurry."

There's no time to argue. I run back to the house. If the Blackjacks come over the hill, at least the outbuildings will hide us until they're right on top of the cellar. I grab the gun. It feels loaded. Hell, what do I know about guns? I grab the bowl in the same hand and carry the candelabra in the other. I hear the Blackjacks running and sliding down the hill behind the barn.

A couple raindrops brush my cheeks.

When I get back to the cellar, the old man is leaning against the door. He's got the key in the lock and he's swearing 'cause he can't turn it. I kneel down and twist it. I lift him up, away from the door, and pull it open.

CHAPTER THIRTY-SIX

BONE CELLAR

The cool dark of that cellar slides up at me. My head spins. The old man is gone. No, he's hobbling down the last step. I throw the candelabra down the stairwell, not even caring if it gets bent up. I turn and stare at the corner of the barn, holding the gun up. I hear footsteps.

"No," the old man says. "Get down here. Now."

"Not down there. Not again." I keep my back turned away from the cellar, facing the corner of the barn.

"You must."

It's like the blackness is grabbing at my feet. I'm sinking.

"No, I can't go down there."

"You're already down, child. Just reach up and close the doors. You can use the same padlock to lock it from the inside latches."

"No way. I'll just stay at the bottom here, with the doors open, and the gun, and face them."

There's flickering candlelight behind me. I see purple and

gold out of the corner of my eye. This, I got to check out. Turning. Dizzy.

White.

The walls, the ceiling, even the floor is whitewashed. A white that pounds my headache. Then it's the shadows. All the shadows flickering in the candlelight.

There's an altar covered in purple cloth even though it's not Lent. Then I see the gold. A cross, a chalice, candlesticks, everything a dull gold against that purple. It's no shiny fake stuff. There's like a window, a crystal, in the middle of the cross. In the window are two twisted yellow bones. I know it's human bones because nothing else makes sense in such a big-deal thing as that cross. It's a relic.

"Take the padlock off the outside latch and close the door." He's facing the altar so his wheezy voice just whispers off the stones.

"Right." I take the lock off the outside and pull the heavy door up and over. I don't know how the old man could have been doing this all these weeks. I hear footsteps running on gravel. A drizzle brushes my face as I let the door drop shut and clamp the lock through the metal latch on the inside.

A body thumps against the outside of the door. Then voices from outside:

"Sonofabitch, I almost had 'em."

"The old man down there?"

"RJ. I saw RJ down there."

"RJ? Shit, this is better than I thought."

"The old man, he's gotta be down there, too. Let's check out the house. It's ours again."

"What about them?"

"They ain't going nowhere."

Sound of footsteps on dirt, then jumping on the porch.

I turn back to the room. It's smaller than I remember it, maybe 'cause it's all crowded what with the altar and the two of us and some blankets that got that funky wet wool smell, and my brain slides me back to being locked in Father Speckler's coat closet on a rainy day, whiffing peanut butter and Free-toes, the sound of water dripping off yellow raincoats, my nose against the bottom of that door, sucking air and listening to Father Speckler droning on about *all God's children*, which I wasn't 'cause I'm like Mother Catherine said, out of bounds to the Lord . . .

"RJ! Take slow, deep breaths." The old man wheezes, bringing me back to the here and now.

I take slow, deep breaths and squeeze the key. The sounds of splintering wood, gonzo laughter, and a wolf howl drift through the rain and down the air vent into the here and now.

"It's time, RJ, for you to hear my confession."

"I ain't a priest."

"That is your finest qualification."

The old man turns over, lying on the moldy wool blanket with his head against the altar. He breathes in soft rattles, like a baby's breath. I kneel on the edge of the blanket. If he can hear the sounds coming from the house, he don't give a sign.

"Now I will tell you my tale. Then you will help me die. Shhh, do not answer, child. I was born in France on April tenth 1893. I was one of seven children on a small farm in Provence."

Each word, each sentence he says is perfect. Like it's all memorized, and all he's doing is reciting.

"Even as a child I felt alone, distant. But I could sing. A sweet alto who could sustain each note of the kyrie with a clarity that made the monsignor's fat lips tremble. I was sent to the monastery."

His head tilts to the side so that he can stare at me as he's talking, though his eyes look like they're seeing back to that other time.

"Every poor family dreamt of losing one of its burdens this way. The monastery was cold and hard and lonely. For the only time in my life I felt at home."

There's something clear and hard way deep inside the old man, like that creepy old body is just a shell he'll toss away any time he feels like it. I sit back listening, wondering if he'll die with the next word or just rattle on with his tale into forever.

The Old Man's Tale of Festering Horrors and God's Litany

I was ordained at nineteen. Then the Great War began. Nothing in my experience, my faith . . . prepared me for . . . sustained me against . . . the carnage. Oh, I understood the necessity of evil to ensure free will. But what comfort is theology in the face of kneeling brothers massacred at prayer? It broke my faith. I left the priesthood and enlisted in the artillery out of revenge on a God who for me no longer existed. I endured most of the war on a single battlefield, Verdun. Endured kneeling in a concrete bunker that thundered beyond human sound. God's litany, I called it. Lord have mercy upon us.

I tended the carrier pigeons. The birds became my solace . . . releasing them to soar untouched above the carnage. In the bunker, soldiers recognized me as a former priest and approached for spiritual solicitude. I told them I believed in nothing. The bunkers teemed with petty human terrors. Much as a monastery. Soon everyone knew of this former priest who believed in the nothing, who knelt not in prayer but in silence against God's litany. Christ have mercy upon us.

The concrete ceiling cracked above us. The ground rippled below us. Men gathered about me, kneeling defiantly against God's litany. Rumors of our defiance spread across the front as officers, awaiting commands fluttering down in the grasp of my sweet birds, instead unfolded the spiritual ramblings of a . . . a madman. But in our close confines, the officers could not risk the revolt that would follow my court-martial. Lord have mercy on us.

And then the war moved on, and we emerged from the bunkers into the light of a pale sky. Those who had knelt with me now averted their eyes, turned their backs. Prior to the war, Verdun had been fertile farmland edged by woods. Now the landscape was a nightmare of twisted ground, ravaged trees, and unspeakable harvest. So began the burial of the dead. We collected plaque d'identité . . . dog tags to the Americans . . . and dumped corpses in the trenches and filled in the earth. We stole from the dead with impunity . . . a coin, a gold ring, a locket, a crucifix . . .

Units mustered out to the final front. As rain pressed hollows into the soft dirt of the mass graves, less than a hundred of us remained to enter the forest. We wandered the woods, burying charred, mutilated, festering horrors. The smell was such a part of us that we could no longer go into the villages. I joined two of my former celebrants as we hoarded our finds together, making a pact to share equally in the unlikely event of our survival.

One day we stumbled across the roof of a stone chapel buried by mud and debris and overgrown with vegetation. Rather than dig out the chapel, we decided to break through the moldy roof. Of course, I was the one chosen to violate the sanctity. I dropped down the opening, the light from above cutting the chapel in two. I took shallow breaths against the stench that was all the foulness from above become intimate, like a whore's bedroom perhaps. I turned away from the corpse of a priest and gazed upon that altar . . . at the gold cross with a crystal at its apex and bones embedded within that crystal. This relic lay on purple linen, surrounded by these sacraments.

It was the chapel containing the relic reputed to be the toe bones of St. Jerome Emiliani, the patron saint of orphans. I had visited this very chapel as a seminarian. Truly, this vault had been transformed as profoundly as . . . as myself . . .

CHAPTER THIRTY-SEVEN
OUR FATHER

The storm hits with this pounding like stones hammering the roof.

"God's litany." The old man tries to smile, but ends up sucking for air.

"You tell a mean tale."

"Likewise, RJ."

So much in his story I don't understand. Maybe it's grown-up stuff that someday if I get out of this mess I'll look back and figure it out. Or maybe it's a mystery for only him to know. The rain smells like ocean. Like if I went up the stairs, threw open the doors, and stuck my tongue out at the sky, the raindrops would have a kelpy taste.

"I never heard a storm come on so hard and sudden like that." I shiver and take slow, deep breaths.

The old man is shaking. Not big shakes, though. Just hard, small shudders. I can't figure if the shakes come from him trying to push the pain out or hold the life in. Maybe it's both.

He turns over and leans up against the altar. He takes deep breaths, his eyes closed. His face is red and waxy in that candlelight.

"Do you know the Lord's Prayer?"

"Yeah, but . . ."

"Recite it with me. 'Our Father, who art in Heaven, hallowed be thy name . . .'"

I repeat it with him. By the time we both get to "Amen," his voice is hardly even a breath.

Then there's music in the rain. Can the old man hear it, or is it only in my head? His eyes glance up. He hears it. The Blackjacks have a boom box cranked up so that hollow house echoes like a loudspeaker. I laugh as Zep's "Stairway to Heaven" weaves through the rain and slips down the air vent and into my headache. Every lame-ass school dance ends with that song. But now, it's like that music was written just for this hard, pounding storm. Sweet incense smoke rubs at my clothes and slides along the walls, creeping toward the air vent.

"Did your Mr. Sanders tell you 'The Pardoner's Tale'?"

I got this picture of Mr. Sanders sitting on that moldy sofa in front of his trailer, sipping from a mug filled with Jack Daniel's, the YOURE HOOSTE sign hanging over his head. "Yeah. Three dudes go looking for death and this old man tells 'em about this tree and they find gold under the tree and kill each other over it. It was pretty cool."

The music stops. There's no sound from the house. That silence is the creepiest of all.

"Such a fate that brings an old man to find a boy to whom he must bestow a terrible burden, only to discover that boy has prepared his entire life to fulfill such a quest."

I got to kneel right in front of him to hear his words, my ear almost against his nose.

"How wonderfully ironic . . ." That putrid baby's breath voice. He even gurgles, except it's not a happy baby gurgle, more a deep, sad kind of rattle. ". . . that at this moment, for the first time in . . . in years, I wish to live. I will finish my confession."

The Old Man's Tale of the Stolen Horde and God's Children

I knelt in that chapel as though to pray. My eyes adjusted to the amber shadows, and I saw jewelry scattered on the cold stone . . . the rings and bracelets, the silver and gold, the pendants and crucifixes, the pearls and diamonds, the ornate and the simple . . .

Villagers, enduring our world's insanity, had entrusted their precious treasures to a saint of another world. Children's offerings lay among the jewelry . . . shattered dolls, rotted stuffed animals, pathetic toys. How long did I kneel amid their tribute before I became aware of the other two staring down at me, at the treasure? I could not pretend this did not exist. I lifted the wealth up to them. Soon the three of us knelt on the moss beside the chapel staring at the golden cross and chalice, and at the jewelry piled in our helmets like a cruel offering.

We discovered a great oak, split by an artillery shell, a hundred yards from the chapel. We would bury the treasure there and come back for it after the war. The shade clung to my skin, stung my nose. Perhaps that stench was merely the remnant of the blast, but to me that oak embodied all the cruelty that had been and all that would be.

Francois would go for food and drink while Henri and I buried the treasure. A look passed between them, and I knew my fate. It was a greater fortune if divided by two rather than three. But there are times a man may defy fate.

We buried the horde deep in the hollow between the roots. Darkness closed about us as Francois returned. The faint almond scent confirmed my suspicion that the poison was in my wine. I pretended to drink with them, spitting out the wine or tipping it to the ground. I fought against the weariness until they passed out.

They would have killed me, no? If not with poison, then another way. I used this Luger. It is small, but feel how heavy. I shot Henri in the head as he slept. Francois sat up, groggy from wine and sleep. The first shot grazed his arm. The second hit his gut. The third to the chest as he reached toward me finished it.

After the Great War I moved to America. It was many years before I finally returned to uncover the horde. I packed and shipped the treasures to myself in America. Perhaps I hoped to be caught. The jewelry financed my life insurance business in Los Angeles. I bought a small bungalow in the foothills overlooking the San Fernando Valley, isolated from my neighbors. I built a concrete bunker . . . an atomic bomb shelter, the neighbors would someday call it . . . and began secretly celebrating Mass. I longed to rid myself of the holy objects, but they held me in their grasp.

"We ask you to transform us into children so that we may one day enter the Kingdom of Heaven."

Obscene housing tracts besieged me, and I nurtured bougainvillea as a purple veil against the outside world. Earthquakes cracked the bunker; fires raged in the hills; a mudslide buried my neighbor. Yet my iniquity endured the wrath of God.

I had but one brief indiscretion. Clara was a temp at my office, an innocent, though not young—a devout Christian who must have thought she saw some mystery in this older man who could sell insurance and yet dwell outside mundane humanity. Men had no doubt found Clara's elongated limbs and gaunt face unattractive, but I saw only her languid spirituality, a heavenly beauty reminiscent of Goya's saints. She surrendered her purity. When I abandoned her, I lost any hope of redemption. She slipped away, and I never heard from her again.

I read in a magazine that the chapel of St. Jerome Emiliani had been restored, yet the relic remained lost. Ah, the pictures of the empty altar announced my sin to the entire world! I still dreamt of one day placing the gold and crystal and bone back in the amber light of that chapel. Whether I could not let go of the treasure or it would not let go of me, I do not know. But soon a decade passed and I became old. Then another decade passed and all hope was lost.

Two days after my seventy-fifth birthday, a lawyer informed me that I had a son by Clara. The evidence was indisputable, but nothing was demanded of me. He was in his early thirties by that time. She had left it in her will that I should be informed of his existence, nothing more.

Of course, this was fate. If I was too feeble, too corrupt to return the sacred objects, perhaps someone who shared my blood, yet retained some goodness, could complete the task. Imagine my despair upon discovering my son had died before I would have found him. But he had two children, each by a different mother. And so I waited again until they would come of age. How is it possible that at eighty-five I could find the strength to move to this godforsaken farm? Neither of my grandchildren had inherited their grandmother's homeliness, yet both, even in their darkest moments, exuded her spirituality, her purity. Roxanne had been my first hope, but it was not to be her.

So my life ends here with you.

CHAPTER THIRTY-EIGHT

RELIC

My grandfather slumps against the altar, his eyes closed. My grandfather. Looking back, it all fits together, and I feel like a prospect that I hadn't figured it. It makes the kind of sick sense that only happens in this for real world. So why didn't I feel a connection to him? My feelings are like some pearl buried way deep inside me.

Weird sounds slide through the rain outside. Whisperings. Footsteps sloshing mud.

The old man is not breathing. Was that all Roxanne was to him, someone to do his dirty work? Is that all I am to him, some kind of cosmic go-fer? No. There's more to us than that.

I remember taking care of Charley after he was born. He breathed so softly when he slept that I was afraid he'd stop altogether. Sometimes he lay there without moving, even his little chest not bumping up or down, and I'd rush over there, just staring, forcing him with my mind to breathe. Breathe!

Afraid, for some reason, to touch him. Then he'd get a little gurgle in his throat, or he'd ball up a fist, or wiggle feet that even then bulged out against the plastic soles of his sleepers, and only then would my heart jump-start and I'd breathe. The old man looks just like that now.

"Breathe," I whisper. I bend over and listen to his chest . . . a soft, faraway rattle. A clammy hand grabs my shoulder. The claws go around me like a wannabe hug and it's like I'm afraid to move. But then it's like I don't want to move.

"How long was I out?" Grandfather drops his arms.

"A couple minutes." I crawl back away from him.

"Minutes?"

"Yeah. Maybe two, three max."

"A lifetime," he whispers. "A lifetime."

"I hate you."

"Oh, child, if only you did."

There's a long quiet and he drifts off again. I'm trying to force him to breathe with my mind, just like I'd done with Charley. Why am I doing that? Just let him go. He opens his eyes, but I can't see into them through the shadows.

"Do you understand now?"

"No. Understand what?"

"What you must do when I am dead." He nods at the back corner of the cellar, at that worn backpack, brown and crusty with blood. "You must . . . return it."

"I don't get it! What do you want from me?"

"Please forgive me."

"What?"

"Forgive me."

"I ain't God or Jesus or a priest! I ain't nothing! . . . I'm only just RJ."

"Forgive."

He passes out again, only this time my mind don't work at keeping him breathing. My head pounds. I pop a couple more aspirins. That sorry, crippled old man is my grandfather. I figure he can't hear me, so I say it.

"Grandfather, I forgive you . . . I forgive you for . . . for all the stuff you did . . . and also for all the stuff you should have done but didn't. I forgive you."

His eyes open.

"You tricked me, you old . . ."

I can hardly tell the grin from all the other wrinkles on his face.

"In one of your tales," he whispers, "your mother said you had a sweet voice just like your father. I wish I could have heard his voice."

"I think I remember it even though I was only just three."

"Sing for me."

"I don't sing."

"I never knew of my son's . . . your father's . . . voice until you told your tale. It is our voices that connect us."

"After my mom said about my father having that same sweet voice, I didn't sing no more songs. There are no songs inside me."

Pictures in my head, almost like someone else, of my first Communion. Of that little children's choir. *Yes, Jesus loves me . . .*

"I don't remember no songs."

He's just lying there, his head propped up. I can feel his eyes studying me from inside the candlelight shadows.

Yes, Jesus loves me . . .

"I won't sing." It's like the song is all twisted up, sliding around, trying to find its way out like that incense toward the air vent.

"For our first solo," he wheezes, "'Ave Maria' had been requisite."

"I don't know that song," I lie. "I just know that kids' one, 'Yes, Jesus Loves Me.'"

He winces, like the title could kill him. "Don't you know something not quite so . . . innocent . . . so cloying?"

"There's nothing wrong with that song." I don't know why I'm POed at him bagging on a song I don't even want to sing in the first place.

And then the tune slides out of my gut just to spite him. *"Jesus loves me, this I know, for the Bible tells me so. Little ones to him belong. They are weak, but he is strong."*

His face scrunches up. The sweeter I sing, the more it hurts him. So I make the notes come out as sweet and pure as I can.

"Yes, Jesus loves me. Yes, Jesus loves me . . ." Singing over and over. *"Yes, Jesus loves me. The Bible tells me so . . ."* Singing over and over, listening to the words bounce off the stones. Listening to them against the warm, steady rain. Singing them as clear and sweet as I can make them. Singing them long after I hear the Blackjacks' gonzo laughter from just outside the air vent. Singing them long after I know my grandfather is dead.

I lay his body out on the floor, cross his arms on that old suit, and cover him with the blanket.

Something heavy crashes against the cellar door.

Grandfather wanted me to return this relic. But how can I do that when I can't even get out of here? He said something about remembering "The Pardoner's Tale." The gun lies next to me on the stone floor. Than a plan slaps into me.

Another smash against the door.

I move fast now. Grab the backpack and pick only the holy objects to stuff in it. The last thing I put in is the cross with the saint's toe bones stuck in the crystal. I take what Father Speckler would have called the secular objects, jewelry mostly, and lay it at grandfather's feet, where it'll be seen from above. I can't believe how much of it there is. Just a couple of these pieces . . . that gold ring with diamonds and that green stone that looks like a for real emerald . . . They could get my mom out of all her jobs. They could . . . All it would take are a couple of pieces in my pockets. I lift the pack on my back. Man, it's heavier than Charley and that old man put together.

Some kind of boulder thunders against the door. God's litany.

I pick up the gun and turn to meet them.

The wood splits apart and the heel of a boot crashes through.

"Damn, I'm stuck. Pull me back."

The boot disappears. There's shouts and then a rain of splinters as the door shatters. I guess I knew a long time ago, maybe from the sounds, that there's only three of them left. The Ace and his two sidekicks.

I aim the pistol at his chest as he steps down the stairs. He laughs, probably figuring that little thing is a toy. Then he stops laughing. He's lifting the stone he used to bash in the door. My finger tightens on the trigger. He stops. That open door behind them makes my head spin and I fight down the urge to bolt past them and up the steps. He lowers the stone to the floor. I suck in the clean air and bide my time, like they say. They bend over to fit under that ceiling. Any one of them could reach out a long, freckly arm and grab the Luger.

"That gun must be sixty years old." The Ace laughs again, but now it's more forced. "It won't never . . ." His mouth drops open. He's seeing all the gold and jewels for the first time. It's like my gun goes clear out of his mind and he just stares.

"Kinda pathetic," I say, "a hundred years of Blackjacks coming down to you three."

He forces himself to look up from that loot. He's just a strung-out punk.

"We're on our last deal," I say.

"What deal is that?"

"You guys step back up the steps, and I won't pull this trigger. And don't say no dumb-ass movie talk about how I don't got the guts to do it, 'cause truth is I don't know if I got the guts NOT to do it."

He twitches and my hand jerks, almost pulling the trigger. They scramble back, pushing and shoving and swearing, but never taking their eyes off the stash.

It's my turn to laugh.

They step back from the door. I climb up the stairs, the heavy backpack tugging at the nerves in my neck and yanking at my brain like it could pull me back down.

There's only a light rain now. The three of them stare at me like I'm full-bore gonzo. But they only stare for a second, 'cause their eyes go back down the steps to the treasure.

"Here's how it goes," I say. "I'm just gonna back around here. Then I'll let you go down there. The gold is yours."

They nod, but they're not really listening. They don't even see my backpack. I back away, and they're fighting each other to be the first down the steps. They're even pushing the Ace out of the way like he's nobody, and I know that the Blackjacks are undone.

I take one last look to make sure they're not touching my grandfather's body. But they're too busy with the gold. I throw the gun down the stairs. It belongs down there.

CHAPTER THIRTY-NINE
BABY'S GRAVE

I climb up the hill behind the house, slogging through weeds and mud. The rain stops. The open air fills me, blowing my headache clean away.

My pockets are empty of any of that secular horde. Somehow, my grandfather knew they would be. But the weight of carrying all this church gold . . . just one piece . . . maybe that gold chalice that drips with the little red stones like for real blood drops . . . Just one piece would free my family. One piece would maybe fix Charley's toes. What good is it to a church that's already got more gold than it knows what to do with?

I sit at the top of the hill. Sun rays split the high clouds, dancing over fields already gone green, glistening off metal roofs. I'm sitting at the same spot as on that night when all this began . . . Roxanne with her chin on her knees smearing that purple polish across her toenails . . .

I pull the heavy cross out of the pack. What am I going to

do with it? Grandfather wanted me to return it to its chapel. But how can I do that? It's not like I can just make a house call off in France somewhere. Maybe I should tell my mom all about it. Except she sucks at making the right choices. Then what about asking Abuelita? It hits me, what she'd said about Charley. *He has the toes of a saint.* Maybe she had been talking about more than just Charley's toes. But if I asked her, she'd just tell me another story, so I'd have to figure it out myself anyway. Okay, so maybe I just haul it down to the mission—that's easy enough. After all, that's almost like taking it to its for real chapel. Same outfit, anyway. But I've trusted priests before, and it didn't ever turn out like I'd planned.

A muffled clap from inside the root cellar bounces up the hill. A gunshot. But there's nothing I can do about that.

So maybe the cross has the answer. If it really holds some holy relic, it ought to have a bunch of miracles stashed away inside. I set it on a boulder in the grass. It's a dull gold that sucks up the sunlight. I stare into that crystal like it's a freaking TV screen into the future. I can see through to the world on the other side, the grassy hill streaked in funny colors, the barn twisted into weird shapes. The bones inside look smooth and yellow. Even if a lot of these relics were just con jobs, it gives me the willies thinking some guy had these toes hacked off his foot. He might have been a for real saint, or he might have been a murderer, or he might have just been a regular guy.

Another clap bounces up the hill.

This relic is one of the most awesome things I ever seen, but there's no miracle in it for me. It makes me sick sitting here waiting for some quick fix when I got a job to do. Grandfather wanted me to return it . . . but he didn't say when. I lift it and stuff it back in the pack. I shoulder the weight and just start walking. The mission bell tolls Mass, but I'm heading away from any of that up into the hills.

Just walking and walking until I'm climbing up Dead Man's Gorge. The relic tugs at me like a whole lot of Charleys. Walking on the muddy path above purgatory. The hatch is open and a mudslide has filled its belly. It will be completely buried soon. Lupine and poppies and mustard spread across the hills. Big Mama rests along the coast with her jugs sticking straight up into low clouds. She's not brown no more, but such a green that makes me want to roll and get lost in her.

A rotted blanket lies in the shade of a boulder, a broken platform dangles from a tree. Cigarette and candy wrappers swirl in the breeze. But no one is here, only silence. I pick up a shovel half buried next to a collapsed tent and continue walking. I climb over the rise and there it is in front of me, its branches creepy fingers against a clean sky. The rattan chair has blown away over the cliff. The evil is broken. The two roots are open arms.

Could there already be something buried there?

I stand between them and shrug off the backpack and drive the shovel into the earth. This wooden handle, this blade sucked by mud, this hole opening under me are all I know. This hole now deep as a baby's grave.

But it's only just a hole. Nothing more.

I bury the backpack with every piece of that sacred gold.

Someday, when I'm old enough, I'll return and dig it out and return the relic to its chapel. But for now it's got to rest here. No one will mess with it. I turn and head home.

A part of me already misses the weight that won't ever be on my back again.

AUTHOR'S NOTE

Arcangel Valley—its people, places, and events—are a figment, as RJ would say. But he also said, "When it comes right down to it, made-up parts have the most for reals in them." Of course, our world in the year 1978 often intrudes within its boundaries. At such times, I have strived to make an accurate account of that era, with a few liberties—and I'm sure, a few mistakes.

The concept and imagery of relics embodies the venal and the spiritual, the morbid and the exquisite. I mean no disrespect to anyone's beliefs. St. Jerome Emiliani is, to the best of my knowledge, the patron saint of orphans in the Catholic Church. However, the particular relic mentioned in this book, as well as the chapel in which the reliquary was housed, are entirely fiction.

I wish the same could be true for the Battle of Verdun—and all battles, with their horrors that spill beyond their own bloody ground and wash down through time.

ACKNOWLEDGMENTS

Mom and Dad, how I wish you could be holding this book now.
To my wife and children, my everything.
To my sister, Heather, the first to have ever heard my stories.
To Sheila Finch, lifelong friend and mentor. And to Dan Houston-Davila, whose enthusiasm for literature and life has swept me in its wake. In memory of one of my oldest friends, a fellow teacher and writing companion, Harry Lowther. And to all the other members of the Asilomar crew, founded by Jerry Hannah, especially: Rose Hamilton-Gottlieb, Dave and Mary Putnam, Jon Russ, Barry Slater, Kendall Evans, Natalie Hirt, Lydia Bird, Paul and Judy Bernstein, Susan Vreeland, and Samantha Henderson. What a long, strange trip, my friends.

To Stephen Barr, the greatest of agents. Without your "yes" I truly believe this book would never have found a home. When I sit with other writers and they commiserate about agents, they are envious when I describe your devotion to your craft. Your belief in *Bones of a Saint* (a nod to your

ACKNOWLEDGMENTS

contribution of said title) willed it into existence. Thank you, my friend. And also to all the others at Writers House, for their work and support. Someday I hope to visit and maybe go in that mysterious vault and, who knows, find *Bones* there. Though I'm not sure how RJ would feel being trapped in a small, dark place.

To Daniel Ehrenhaft, editor extraordinaire and a great advocate of this book. It felt as though RJ and Daniel were good friends from the beginning. A visionary, indeed. And to Rachel Kowal, the managing editor tasked with somehow accepting RJ's odd voice and rendering it onto the page. And to all the team at Soho, not only for publishing this novel, but for keeping storytelling alive.

Finally, to all who partake in the communion of tales.